Edited by Linda Nagle



Published in Great Britain in 2020 by Matthew Cash/Burdizzo Books, Walsall, UK

TESCO a-go-go MATTHEW CASH

**Burdizzo Books**

**2020**

# Foreword

When I first came to Walsall, my girlfriend at the time took me to The Trough. She banged on about this infamous rock pub in her letters all the time and wanted to show me its delights. I'd never been to a rock pub before. Most of the ones I had been to up until then had been your generic country pubs where the most you could get to eat was a bag of crisps and a packet of dry roasted, Then there were the bars of Ipswich where you almost always had to wear sensible shoes and dress smart-casual. I was excited. I was a big rock and metal fan and never knew such places existed, but coming from rural Suffolk meant I was very naive in a lot of things.

Although the place blared loud rock music and the clientele seemed to be a mixture of street urchins and Hell's Angels, I loved how comfortable it felt and how nobody really gave a shit what you looked like. These 'scary' looking people were welcoming to everyone, not just those who fit in with their scene. There was an unspoken mutual respect amongst everyone: treat people how you want to be treated.

I soon came to love the place. It was somewhere I could go to relax and I didn't have to worry about going home and getting changed or anything other than the money in my pocket. It was somewhere I could go and not get picked on for being a weirdo.

I had loads of silly drunken exploits in this place, which I can still see from my window. Legendary nights of excessive drinking of Newcastle Brown Ale; the most I managed in one night was twenty bottles before I fell asleep in the beer garden on a picnic bench and everyone played buckaroo with the empty bottles. The girls I pulled (I don't know how the fuck that happened) well, someone did once say that I had a way with words. It sure as shit couldn't have been my looks!

It was during my years spent there or at work that I started writing about 'real' stuff for the first time in my life. Everything else I had written up until then had some form of monster in it and I think I just wanted to get the place down on paper.

The friendship is what I had always longed for and what I temporarily had. Everyone who has gotten to know me will know how I had a best mate, and we had just as much fun as Dave and Ian do in this book—and how women and stubbornness ended our friendship after ten years. Even though it's been five years, I still miss him. I miss those mental nights where we were both so skint we had little else to do than drink supermarket brand pop and dance to music like idiots until we fell asleep. I doubt I'll ever find another friend I could get as close and comfortable with, and that's a shame—but it's just the way it is. So mostly, this book is for him and I'm hiding it here so those who don't read forewords will miss it. He's an avid reader and used to be my best mate, so who knows? Mark Somerfield, this book is for you and I'm sorry for all the times I was a cunt.

The Trough served me well, it helped me celebrate during my relationships and my marriage, comforted me when those ended, and even though my drinking days are over for the time being, it's still somewhere I know I'd feel welcome. I hope.

Matty-Bob
2020

## Dedication

This book is dedicated to people and a building.

To try and name everyone who played a part in fuelling the embers that became this book is virtually impossible; As with any great pub that you frequent enough, sometimes you only know these people by sight. You know the types of people, the ones who are like genies that live at the bottom of beer bottles and only ever appear when you're off your tits. The next day or during the working week you'd be walking through town and someone you'd swear on the lives of your nearest and dearest that you had never laid eyes on would nod at you as you passed them by with a look of confusion. Either that or it would be a mutual vague recognition, where both you and the stranger thought you knew one another but weren't quite sure where from, especially if you were both in work clothes or your personality wasn't showing.

The first part of this dedication is to those people, real and imaginary, the gin genies, those I've only ever spoken to whilst pissed and had no recollection of thereafter. I'm sorry if I was a twat or broke your heart or something like that.

The second part of the dedication is for the bar staff of this immortal pub, and it really is immortal. No matter how many times it gets knocked down (figuratively speaking) it always seems to bounce back. I've not seen it in its latest incarnation but I've heard great things from those who were there back in the day, back in *my* day.

The barmaids really were fucking badass bitches and they are exactly as described in this book. They were all drop dead gorgeous and could kick the living shit out of you if you gave them any lip at last orders. Some of what you will read in this book, of the main character's reaction to one particular barmaid is exactly how I felt about one of the servers in the pub. I literally could not go to the bar if she was serving as she was far too hot for me to speak to. I wasn't worthy.

So, the barmaids, apart from 'The One' who I shall refuse to name, although one of the named barmaids knows exactly who it is.

Holly (who had the loudest gob and an amazing, AMAZING arse) is now one of my biggest fans and our daughters don't stop talking about Animal Crossing. (I am far too much of a gentleman to see if the arse is still doubly amazing but I bet it is.)

Jodie, who was like a little pixie and I fancied her rotten but she never found out until I just wrote it here. She also rocks and loves the Matty-Bob books.

Kelly another barmaid who kicked arse and who, to be honest, I was a little bit scared of. I still *am*, a little, sometimes we're in the gym together.

And last but not least, Wills, technically he was one of the barmaids too. He put up with hours of my shite during lock-ins and now on occasion we torture one another in the gym.

The third and final part of the dedication is to the friends I can name. Friends that I met in The Trough and friends that I practically lived in there with. Some have come and gone as friends do but as they all played a part, even if it was after this book was written, they deserve to be recognised. They all have special connections in my memory and this place.

Reece, Monique, Billie, Samantha, Ollie, Helena, Ange, Marc, Skottii, Lisa, Rob and finally Mark for being the Ian to my Dave for ten hilarious years. For those I'm not in touch with, I hope life is treating you well. For everybody, try and get through 2020 – hopefully 2021 won't be standing behind it saying, "hold my beer."

Cheers, Motherfuckers!

## Chapter 1: Soufflés

Sexy girls! Sexy *naked* girls! Sexy naked *lesbian* girls! In *custard! With horns!* Sexy naked lesbian girls with horns in a king-size *swimming pool* of custard! *Wrestling!* And Dave was their master. A master who stood poised like an Olympian diver wearing nothing apart from swimming goggles and a look of grim determination. He was the Bitchfinder General. Only he could cure these hellions from their unholy cavorting in the dairy products made from the milk from Satan's teats.

The sexy naked horned lesbians in custard looked up from their nude custardiness. "Behold," they cried in unison, "Our Master Davidian of The Steel Rod is here!"

They wanted to be saved and he wanted to save them. With his penis.

Dave gazed upon them and wiped a lock of his long black hair away from his blue eyes. He spoke in a deep, dark voice—not unlike the late Peter Steele of Type O Negative. "I, Davidian of the Steel Rod, must undertake the fate with which life has cursed me. Every day, for all eternity, I must wrestle, cavort and copulate with each and every one of you. I shall save you. I will guide you onto the holy path. With my penis."

"Take us, Master," Came the chorus of sexy naked lesbian girls in custard. Dave stepped onto the white diving board and got ready to jump.

*What was that?*

A high-pitched beeping noise. He looked at the vision of ecstasy before him and dived...

"Fucking arseholes!" Dave said, reaching for the mobile phone that beeped beside him. Why the hell did he always have to wake up at *that* point?

He switched off the infernal racket and threw it on to the cheap IKEA bedside cabinet. Now, if he remembered correctly, he still had an extra half-hour in bed and the dream had left him in a rather extreme state of arousal. He lifted up his duvet and stared at his erection, straining against his boxer shorts with a rather fetching wigwam effect.

*Would it be possible for it to tear through the material?*

"What a fucking waste," he said to his cock as he released it from its underwear prison. "If only those sexy naked custard lesbians were real, there'd be more than enough of you to go around, wouldn't there?"

His penis, unsurprisingly, didn't answer. Had it the ability to be able to think or speak it would have suggested that Dave put on his *Babes Illustrated* video and take it in hand, as it was going to be no use to anyone if it was left straining itself like this. But uncannily as it may seem, Dave had these exact thoughts, picked up his video remote control and flicked a couple of buttons. Within seconds his vision was filled with a pair of women participating in unspeakable acts of obscenity.

*

Stella looked remarkably young for her fifty-two years, with her strawberry-blonde hair in a funky, short style. Bob, who was two years older than his wife, had one of the world's shiniest bald heads. As the vicar of St Martin's, members of his congregation would often make jokes about the time the sun shone through the church windows during one of his sermons, illuminating his head with an apparent halo.

Stella and Bob considered themselves young at heart and were always telling people about their various exploits: line-dancing, rock climbing, hang-gliding, power walking—and going to the Christian theatre.

At this moment, they were preparing for their infamous Saturday dinner. Once a week, they would get together with their circle of friends and take turns in cooking. It was nothing short of a competition - each couple would pull out all the stops to create a meal more elaborate than the previous week's effort, and there would be a vote for the couple who would be crowned culinary king and queen. It was Stella and Bob's turn today—so far, they were twelve points in the lead. It was supposed to be a bit of fun, but some had been known to take things too seriously.

Today's menu was even more lavish than their last. The starter was to be carrot soufflé in a coriander and parsley sauce, followed by salmon and Camembert parcels with a lemongrass and mushroom marinade.

The brioche was a side order, of course.

Dessert was going to be one of Bob's own creations: *White Chocolate Wonder,* a ginger-and-syrup sponge with a biscuit base, coated in a thick white chocolate casing. All to be washed down with several bottles of a wine from Southern France—Chateau De Gainsbourg was regularly delivered to their house.

Stella and Bob had one child, a son. He was at the University of Birmingham studying to become an English teacher. They didn't get to see him much during term time, poor boy. Nevertheless, Stella kept in touch; luckily for him, his parents paid his mobile phone bills.

Stella checked on the soufflés and walked over to the white telephone upon the white kitchen top in the pristine white kitchen. "I'm just going to give David a quick ring, let him know we still love him and all that," she said, reaching for the receiver. "Can you keep an eye on my soufflés?"

"Yes, dear."

*BRRIIING!*

"Oh sugar," shrieked Stella, "they're here already!"

"Calm down, dear, I'll let them in. Put the phone on loudspeaker, then you'll be able to check on the dinner and we can all say hello to David. Get all our friends to embarrass him."

Stella laughed at the thought. "What a lovely idea. You let them in, then, and I'll check the soufflés and give him a call." As she checked on the starters, she could hear seven different voices coming down the hallway. The loudest was John—who called everyone *old boy,* even though he was the oldest of the lot.

Bob ushered everyone into the kitchen. "I know this isn't our usual routine, but Stella's on the phone to our baby boy, David, and we thought it'd be nice for him to hear some friendly voices from home." There were choruses of "Oh, isn't that nice!" from the ladies, and "He doesn't want to hear us old codgers!" from the men.

Stella smiled and put her finger to her lips when David picked up. "Hello, son, this is your mother, I just thought it'd be a nice idea to give you a quick call as we're having our usual Saturday lunch—we thought it'd be nice for a few old friends to say hello!" Stella gestured to the group. The room filled up with shouts of "Hello, old boy, " and "Hope you're studying hard." They all listened for a reply, but none came.

"He's in shock, poor boy," said John. "Told you he wouldn't want to hear us old codgers." Everyone broke into laughter.

"She, " Stella said, "I can hear something."

A voice spoke from the phone. "*What a fucking waste, if only those sexy naked custard lesbians were real, there'd be more than enough of you to go around, wouldn't there?*"

*

Dave took his penis in hand, eyed the obscene acts of lesbian pornography that his Sharp television was exhibiting before him, and began to masturbate furiously. Grunts and groans from Dave and the two lesbians filled the room. He was getting more and more worked up.

The thing that pissed Dave off about pornographic videos was that they always had to make conversation mid-fuck. Especially when it was a man and woman, the man kept shouting things like, "Suck *that* cock, bitch," and making noises like an American wrestler. Why did they have to refer to their genitalia in the second person? This video was particularly irritating as all the speech was in German. He tried to focus on the visual side of the video but found it off-putting when one of the busy girls looked up from her meal and said something like, "Gibt es etwas, was man nicht essen kann?"("Is there anything you can't eat?")

And what was it with the music in pornos? It seemed to Dave's vast experience that the more shit the music, the harder the porn. It was getting heated now, though, the silly German lezza had quit the dodgy script and was getting down to the good stuff. Dave wouldn't be able to last much longer. This was his favourite video and he never lasted long after the blonde one got the baby oil out. The sight of the two wriggling, their writhing supple bodies sliding against each other was too much for him to take, and he came *extremely* loudly. "Oh, fucking hell, yes, yes, yes urrrgghh..." He sprayed sperm all over the sheets beside him and some even landed on his bedside cabinet.

"Oh shit," he thought, "I hope I haven't got any on my phone." He reached across and picked up his mobile phone. There was none on it, thank god. It was his third mobile, the previous one had fallen down the toilet.

How embarrassing would it be to say he'd broken his new one by getting spunk in it? As he checked it for globules, he saw something that chilled him down to the marrow. There was a name on the screen. Which meant that not only had someone rung him but that they were STILL on the line! It couldn't have been his alarm making that noise. The phone had been ringing! "Oh, fucking fucker's fuck," Dave thought. "What the hell should I do now?"

*

Stella sat on the kitchen floor in a state of impenetrable shock. Her husband and visitors stood likewise. All apart from John, who muttered, just before he was cut off by a slap from his wife, "I think I've got that vid..."

"Hello, Mum?" came a voice from the phone.

Stella screamed, burst into tears, and ran from the room.

*

Dave ended the call. Why did he have to say, *Hello, mum*? He didn't know which was worse, the fact that he had just masturbated in earshot of his parents, or the fact that the call had lasted one-and-a-quarter minutes. He sighed and put his face in his hands, forgetting about the sticky substance that coated one of them. "Oh, fucking fuck."

And so began another day in the life of David Smith.

# Chapter 2: The Importance of Being Honest

Dave Smith was a diehard rock fan. He adored it all, everything from Anthrax to Zeppelin, from Anal Cunt to Graveworm. Being a diehard rock fan was almost on par with a religious movement. Compulsory hair growth for men - let it all grow, from as many orifices as possible. Dave had shoulder-length blond hair that was in dire need of a wash and a ginger beard that made him look like kissing cousins to an orangutan. In his right ear, he had two rings, and another in his right eyebrow. He wore clothes of the rock persuasion: baggy black jeans over Doc Martens, and an original 1970 Black Sabbath t-shirt he had found in a charity shop.

Dave cruised along the Walsall pavement, chomping through a bag of Scampi and Lemon Nik Naks. He was walking down the street known as Bridge, past the many, many, *many* takeaways. He had often wondered just how many takeaways there were in this particular town. It was amazing that out of all the millions of eateries infesting this certain street, there were only about two that weren't either a kebab shop or pizza place.

The street stunk of stale junk food and was forever filthy—especially on a weekend morning. A deluge of discarded beer cans, half-eaten pizzas, and puddles of peach-coloured vomit coated the pavements and adorned the entrances to bars and pubs. Dave loathed the nightlife in this town. Dress codes everywhere and their dreadful music tortured his ears. His only small sanctuary was a pub called *The Rising Sun*, which was known locally by its former name, *The Trough*. One of an unholy trinity of rock pubs in Walsall and it was simply the best, to quote Tina Turner.

Past the sweet shop he went, ignoring the unwashed guy in the blue puffer jacket who always asked him for seventy-five pence. Why seventy-five pence? One of the unknown mysteries of all time. Forget Atlantis. Forget the Bermuda triangle. Is there a Loch Ness monster? *Who gives a fuck?* Why Rigsby, the wall-dwelling trampy bloke wants seventy-five pence off everybody, now *there's* a mystery begging to be unravelled. And little did Dave know that he was going to find out the answer, one day soon (but unfortunately, not in this story).

He crossed over the road outside the latest in late night meat markets, a nightclub called Studio 45 which seemed to be full of underaged teens, leery old men, and groovy old grannies who tested the strongest strength of beer goggles.

Past the Greek restaurant that always reeked of cabbage, due to some drainage problem and the fact that a million years ago Walsall decided to put a road over a river. Dave walked into a shopping arcade, The Old Square.

Dave worked in Tesco—and he hated it. It was the cesspit of evil and it overflowed with putrid pieces of shit who, in the retail world, were referred to as *customers.* But unlike the customers that frequent a music store or a book shop, the ones you got in this place were the lowest of the low, the thickest of the thick, the twattiest of the twatty, and so on and so forth. Everywhere you looked, your vision would be polluted. Teenage mums in sportswear, their ears dragged down with colossal golden-hooped earrings, and ghastly, action-figure sized clown pendants on cheap chains around necks stained green by cheap jewellery. Alongside these dwellers of the shit pit the male of the species would stumble, their plumage similar, slouching and slurring in their Neanderthal behavioural patterns. All had the look of the dim-witted about them.

These are known as *Chavs.*

There was the occasional normal person about, even some good-looking people, and the odd Goth dotted about here and there. But if you put too much manure on your flower bed, you're not going to see the roses through the shit.

Dave changed into his uniform and prepared for a full afternoon of doing as little as possible with his one true friend. His friend, who had one of the world's coolest names. *What's so goddamn cool about the name Ian?* You ask. Well, how about if you find out his surname is *Maiden*? Ian Maiden! EXCELLENT!

Ian Maiden was a devotee of rock, just like his soul mate, Dave. But whether it be his curse or his blessing, Ian's favourite band was… yup, you guessed it. Quite accustomed to brushing off the jokes and sniggers by now, he wore his official t-shirts with pride, and when he was in his uniform, he would always have his Maiden tattoo over his heart.

The pair were standing in the darkest corner of the Tesco warehouse, above the shop floor.

"So, what have we got written down so far?"

Ian, a large man two years older than Dave, read from his notebook. "Standing on a lightning-lit mountain peak, over the thunderclaps and hurricanes bawling, over the howls of the wolves, I hear your voice calling."

Dave smiled. "That's cracking," said he.

Ian scratched his scruffy black mane, deep in thought, as he read and re-read the lyrics before him. It was their mission to write the bestest rock song in the whole wide world. He was brought out of his concentration by Dave rustling something on the shelf. A packet of prawn cocktail-flavoured crisps appeared before his eyes.

"Behold!" Cried Dave, "a gift from the gods!"

Ian accepted the packet and stared at the floor solemnly. "I am but a poor peasant man, I thought, not worthy was I of such a miraculous token, given by the gods to whom I did pray! I accept your gift, O mighty Davidian!"

Snatching away the notebook, looking a little embarrassed, Dave said, "Right, where were we? I think it'd rock if these first four lines were spoken with just a solitary bell tolling in the background. Then get this really, really loud..."

Dave suddenly became aware of another presence at the end of the aisle.

Standing at their only exit was a vision of viciousness, the epitome of evil. It was the Devil himself, the master of malevolence, the baron of badness, the doctor of depravity, the wizard of wickedness, the dictator of the diabolic, known by many names, the most common of them Cunt. Also known as Manager, John Goode (whose middle name began with a 'B'). He towered over them at an unmeasured height, tall and dark-haired, with a broom for a moustache. He stood staring at the two of them—his legendary stare could loosen the most constipated of bowels. "WHAT THE HELL DO YOU THINK YOU TWO ARE DOING?" He bellowed with such force that a partially-opened bag of M&Ms spilt its contents onto the cold concrete floor.

It was as if Dave and Ian had been whizzed back in time and were facing an angry headmaster. They both did that thing that naughty kids do—looking everywhere apart from the face of the teacher.

Dave was the first to speak. He knew it'd be a long shot, but at least he tried, bless him. "Getting some stock?"

Goode's face grew red and he screamed at the top of his voice, "Getting some stock? You were stealing, boy. Stealing."

Both Dave and Ian started doing that *other* thing kids do, fidgeting with everything in reach.

Goode took a step closer.

*Oh well,* thought Dave, *I'll just have to sign on again, and sponge off the parents for the six weeks I'll have to wait to get paid because I was sacked. I'll be fine. But what about Ian?* He was on his own; he had no family to sponge off. It was up to him to do something. He couldn't let Ian go down for a bag of prawn cocktail crisps! (Dave actually knew of a girl who would go down for a bag of prawn cocktail crisps, by the way, The Trough was *that* sort of pub.)

Dave looked Goode in the eyes and shouted, "No, you filthy bastard, I won't do it!"

Goode's angry face transformed into one of bewilderment.

Dave whispered something to Ian. He pushed past the manager and ran.

"What on Earth are you going on about, boy?" Goode said. "Where's he going?"

Dave could hear other voices coming into the warehouse. "No, I won't do it. I don't care if you sack me." He lunged forward into the manager, yanking down the zip on his flies, and fell to his knees. Goode's immediate reaction was to slap Dave round the head. Just as he did this, Ian and two other Tesco team members came into the warehouse.

The scene played out before them. The all-powerful Mr. Goode, flies open, a young man on his knees, being slapped around for something he desperately did not want to do, was evidence enough.

It would be incriminating.

Goode was the last person to cotton on to what was 'going down' and by the time he had, it was too late to talk his way out of it.

## Chapter 3: Beelzepub

"We are evil, evil bastards," said Ian, trying his hardest not to laugh. He sat alongside Dave in the best rock pub in town. Each nursed a pint of medicinal lager. And it *was* medicinal. The trauma of the day's events had deemed it so.

Dave, Ian and the two warehouse operatives who had witnessed what they thought had been an indecent act, sat in the managerial office with Goode and discussed their immediate future.

The 'victim,' Dave, had settled on all four of them having two weeks' paid holiday and a permanent pay rise of one-pound-fifty an hour.

Goode reluctantly agreed to this, on the condition that no one else became involved. And the four Tesco team members left to celebrate. Little did they know that when they got back at the end of the month, not only would they not have been paid for their two weeks off, but they wouldn't have jobs at all! And Goode knew that he had had the last laugh – his revenge on the shit that was Dave Smith.

The Trough was and still is, a Tudor building, with the traditional black wooden beams, three storeys, and those typical crisscrossed windows. It spread off at the back with a glass-domed roof that was part of an old conservatory. Then up to a three-levelled beer garden, complete with concrete picnic benches, where it was traditional to sit on a Friday and Saturday night.

The top tier was forever lost in a perpetual cloud of marijuana. In all weathers, people would gather there until midnight, when everybody would be drawn indoors for a serious bout of head-banging

The interior was just how an old-fashioned English pub should be, even down to the old black-and-white photographs of the local brewery.

One such photograph was symbolic of a monumental piss-up: a man in the official white coat of a professional beer-taster, drinking a pint of ale. He looked remarkably like a young Harry Secombe (anyone who has seen him play Mr. Bumble, Oliver's orphanage blokey will know who the hell he is). *Geoff Woolend, 1962-1968.* That's all it said, nothing else. It left Dave and Ian dumbfounded. What did it mean? That it took the man six years to drink that very pint? No one knows. Legend had it that the photo and its frame appeared there one night back in '69, and every attempt to remove it had failed.

The pub had its traditional lounge section then a bit of a dancefloor—a little stage where the DJ played metal, and a pool table hidden behind it. Then there were the toilets. So bad, the word 'toilet' is too good to describe them. 'Shit-houses' is probably more apt.

The gents' were forever in two inches of piss, sandbags were often used to prevent it from flooding the dancefloor. The older patrons would jest about donning waders and going to 'pay the ferryman' when going to use them. A solitary toilet bowl sat miraculously intact despite the many spider web cracks over its surface. Any day now, it would be sure to disintegrate beneath some unlucky drunkard.

It was one of those toilets where it didn't really matter whether or not you were too drunk to direct your stream at the target, because you could just do what everyone else does and piss wherever you like, as long as you were in the room labelled 'toilets.'

The ladies' toilets were just the same, minus the urinals. But the punters of The Trough would have it no other way—it was theirs. To some, it was home.

Dave sat with his back to Geoff Woolend, still wearing the same clothes he had been wearing for the last day-and-a-half. Ian sat beside him, his black hair tied up, as usual, wearing an Iron Maiden t-shirt as usual. They both wondered what the night would bring.

A normal night down The Trough for that pair of losers consisted of staring at the barmaid for a good couple of hours, enough to get another week's worth of masturbatory material, getting blind drunk, then going outside to attempt to hit on some Goth girls five or ten years younger than them. Then, after being told to fuck off, they would go back into the pub to head-bang to the likes of Slayer, Slipknot, Sepultura, and top new Norwegian band H.M.S Satanicca.

As mentioned earlier, their nights began with ogling The Barmaid.

To both of them, The Barmaid, whose name they didn't know, and had never mustered the courage to ask, was the most beautiful woman in the world.

She had long blue-and-black striped hair that framed an innocent angelic face. An innocent angelic face that sported a little silver ring in its nose. Her lips, the lips that had done endless obscenely wonderful things to Dave's body— in his dreams, of course—were red, full, and very much like Angelina Jolie's. The Barmaid gazed out of bright blue eyes that were so big she looked like a manga character. She had a very curvaceous figure: pert breasts that occupied Dave's mind for days, thighs to die for. Tonight, she looked stunning as ever, wearing a twelve-inch black PVC mini-skirt over red fishnets, and a tiny black vest that complimented her cleavage and enabled her to show off her navel piercing and the tattoo on her back. Not to mention the one on her right shoulder. That had sealed the deal for Dave. As soon as he'd seen this tattoo, he fell not only in lust with her but in love. The legendary BLACK SABBATH Celtic cross logo.

"You've got to do it, mate," Said Ian, draining the last of his pint.

Dave managed to tear his eyes away from the perfect pint-puller. "What have I got to do?"

"You must strike up a conversation with The Barmaid—and in time, pull her." Ian looked doubtful. "Or at least get to know her name."

"I bet I can guess her name," Said Dave, his eyes once again filled with The Barmaid's sexy tummy. "I'll bet it's something really unusual like Lorelei or fucking Barberella. Maybe Alicia?"

"What if it's something like Janet or Sue?"

"Don't be so fucking stupid," Dave retorted, "Nobody's called Janet or Sue nowadays, dick."

"Johnny Cash sang about a man named Sue,"

"Exactly, it's a man's name. The Barmaid's definitely got a girl's name."

"Alicia Silverstone," said Ian, backtracking the conversation. "Now, there was an extremely shaggable woman."

They sat for a full minute reminiscing over the work of the famous actress, their minds clinging to the images of her as *Batgirl* in the Hollywood flopbuster *Batman & Robin* for at least forty-five of those seconds.

"I reckon she's a Katie or a Sarah; something normal, but still cute," Ian said. With that, he stood, picking up the empty pint glasses. "I'm going to find out."

Dave watched as Ian walked up to the bar and waited to be served. *He'll never do it.*

Ian brought the round over, to an expectant-looking Dave. "Well?"

Ian sat down, drank a mouthful of lager, and spoke slowly. "Her name is...Barbarella!"

Dave spluttered beer over the table. "Fuck off! You're having a laugh, mate. She must have overheard us or something."

"No, honestly. I shit you not. She said her mum was a fan of the film. A bit of a hippy, too."

Dave was astonished. Beer ran freely from the corners of his mouth and down the front of his t-shirt and nothing intelligible would come out even if he was capable of speech.

This must be fate.

*Barbarella*

He guessed that on a whim.

The name just fell out of his mouth, pretty much like his tongue the first time he saw her.

They'd been calling her *The Barmaid in The Troff* for too long. Knowing her name felt like discovering a lost city below his block of flats. This was a major discovery. He *must* have her.

"I must have her," said Dave, wide-eyed.

Ian nodded slowly. "That you must. As soon as we have accomplished this great feat of impossibility, I can make my move to woo K8."

K8 was the object of Ian's desires. For longer than he liked to admit, he had been admiring her from afar. K8 was a girl of gothic gorgeousness. She shimmered from head-to-toe with the same sort of sexiness Viking warriors had.

The best women in The Trough were the ones who had the faces and bodies of angels, the tongues of demons and could stomp heads harder than the toughest of blokes.

K8 could kick ass.

Her long black hair fell down to her very shapely buttocks. She had a beautiful face with pale skin, sweet pink lips, and startling grey eyes.

She was buxom, curves in exactly the right places, once floored some dick for grabbing her tit with one legendary punch, and Ian was in love. She was his height in chunky black *New Rock* boots with red flames on the sides.

He sometimes imagined her wearing only the boots.

*A feisty one, she is,* as Yoda would say.

Ian doubted that tonight (or any other) would be the night that he and Dave got their dream girls.

## Chapter 4: David and His Amazing Technicolour Bile Yawn

"So, first things first," Said Dave, drawing Ian out of his deep, deep thoughts and fantasies of K8, "Obviously, we shall need much, much more of the Old Dutch courage. I propose that we down these and then go on to the harder stuff."

"What, snowballs?"

"Fuck off, I don't want to end up in hospital having my stomach pumped, you crazy mo' fo'!" Cried Dave, hysterically. "I was thinking more along the lines of snakebites."

"You mean Diesel? Half lager, half cider? You must be having a giggle, mate. Last time I got pissed on them, I was talking to a cash point the next day, with people watching me!" Ian remembered the horrific incident well—little children crying at the *funny man*.

Dave sniggered, the scene in his imagination wasn't far from what really happened. "Yeah—I remember you telling me about that. But we must be at an even higher state of pissedness for the challenges that we face." He finished his pint and went to the bar.

As he approached, he saw *her*, pulling a pint. Everything slowed.

The way she squeezed and pulled the pump with one hand while her fingertips gripped the glass in the other. A glimpse of tongue as she smiled.

The way she pursed her lips to blow some stray hair away from her face. Nothing else mattered to Dave. All he could see was her. He hated how utterly defenceless he became in her presence. All he could hear was the intro of Black Sabbath's... erm..."Black Sabbath."

He reached the bar, his heart pounding heavily in his throat. *Barbarella,* The Barmaid, turned exquisitely towards him and spake beautiful words, "Alright, mate, what can I get you?"

Dave couldn't speak. Nothing would come out.

"Are you alright, mate?" Barbarella asked with a frown.

"Hmmph." It may not have been a decipherable word, but at least he had regained the ability to create audio. All he had to do was fine-tune the Neanderthal grunts to actual words and then he'd be fine. *I'd better hurry the fuck up and say something else before she serves someone else. Come on,* he told himself, *stick to one-syllable words, you'll be okay.*

"Can," Dave pushed the words out slowly, "I…Have…Two…Pints…Of…" He took a deep breath. "Snake...Bite, Please?" He let out a big sigh of relief. *Good job, Me.*

Barbarella, frown slowly vanishing from her forehead, said, "Sure, what type of lager and cider do you want?"

*Fuck.* Another question was taking him well out of his comfort zone. He felt his vision waver. Dave licked his arid lips. "Umm, Carling and Blackthorn please, I love you."

Barbarella went to fetch the drinks. Did she hear him or what? Did he actually say it out loud? Was he that pissed already? Beside him, a huge, bearded man in leathers chuckled into his beer. That was evidence enough that he *had* said it out loud. He knew he would never have the courage to say it again. Best pretend he didn't say it in the first place.

She came gliding back toward him, a vision of gothic beauty, and handed him the pints. "Here you are, mate," She smiled. "That'll be five-twenty, please." He dumped the exact change on the bar and turned to make a sharp exit when Barbarella called out to him. "Oh yeah— mate?"

Dave turned quickly back.

"I love you, too."

The beardy man in the leathers couldn't hold back any longer and erupted into gigantic bursts of uncontrollable laughter.

Dave shuffled back to Ian, who looked extremely amused.

"What the hell happened there?"

"Nothing, fuck-off-you-cunt, drink."

Ian had been admiring K8 from afar again, trying his best to be more subtle than his friend. Although a lobotomised lab rat dripping saliva down her cleavage from three inches away would be more subtle in his ways of secret admiration than Dave Smith.

He watched her on the dancefloor as she thrashed and jerked her head in the strictly metal dance move known as *head-banging*. Hair whipping about like a gorgon having a fit. It was raw, tribal, brutal, sweaty, hairy and just plain fucking sexy.

Even though he didn't feel half as drunk enough, he had the urge to untie his hair, usually only untied for washing and moshing, and join her. How he'd love their hair to get tangled up together. The night was drawing on; there wasn't much time left for them to make a move on their ladies. Dave was nowhere to be seen. Ian suspected that the snakebites had gone to his head and that he was either asleep or throwing up somewhere. He would have to find him. Loyalty to friends was paramount. Plus, if he went on a particular route across the dancefloor, he might be forced to squeeze past K8. This time he might even say 'hello.'

Ian stood up and drained his glass. He had to wait a couple of seconds for the swimmy feeling dissipate. He inhaled deeply through his nostrils, something that he did a lot when pissed, thinking it made him more focused, more alert. It never did. He walked into the darkness of the dancefloor, heading straight for K8, who had her back to him. When he got to her he put a hand against her shoulder, to gently ease her out of his way. As soon as he touched her, K8 spun around, grabbed his arm and twisted it behind his back.

"Aargh! You're gonna break my arm, you bitch!"

K8 pushed him away from the dancefloor and marched him to the corridor outside the toilets, her face a picture of rage. "God, you fucking men are all the same! Walking across the dancefloor just so you can squeeze past girls and cop a feel! Do you realise you do that to me every week?"

K8 looked furious. Ian tried not to notice how much sexier she looked when she was angry, especially when that anger was directed at him.

"And don't think I haven't seen you before. Constantly staring at me," she screamed. "God, if you want something, why the fuck don't you fucking ask?"

Ian looked at her in complete bewilderment. What did she mean by that?

"This," K8 said, grabbing a fistful of Ian's best Iron Maiden t-shirt and pulling him towards her. She thrust her mouth against his and forced her tongue between his lips. Her other hand reached down and clutched at his right buttock.

Ian was sure he could feel his spirit floating away from his body. He hovered above himself and could see K8 pinning his body to the wall by means of her exploring mouth. His body looked as though it was having a bloody good time. Ian floated back down into himself before he missed even more. He had often fantasized about kissing K8 but never dreamed he would get to do it. It felt like nothing he had ever experienced before. Sure, he'd snogged a few girls in his time, but none gave back with this amount of passion, most just slapped him. After a fashion, the seemingly eternal kiss ended and K8 smiled up at him. Neither of them said anything for a while, but it was surprisingly Ian who spoke first. "Jesus," he said, "I'm so glad you just did that."

K8 laughed. She had a cute laugh. It sounded very mischievous. "Believe it or not, Ian, I've wanted to do that for ages."

*My God* thought Ian, *she knows my name!*

"Fuck off! What the hell took you so long?"

K8 smiled. "The same thing that you suffer from. How long would it have taken if I had left it to you to make the first move?"

"Long enough for you to get a black Zimmer frame, probably."

They stood smiling at each other for a few seconds. K8 opened her mouth to speak but her voice was lost beneath the loud whoops and cheers coming from the dancefloor. They went back on to the dancefloor and saw that the weekly metal band The Syphilitic Corpses were ready to play. The lead singer grabbed the microphone, a tall, thin bald man, riddled with piercings and tattoos. He said something indecipherable, which ended with "fuckers". They launched into a heavier version of Alice Cooper's "Hey Stoopid," as Ian and K8 joined in with the raucous rabble of rocking rascals jumping.

As the second song ended, Ian put his mouth to K8's ear. "I'm going to go and see where my mate's disappeared to. I ain't seen him for hours and I'm quite worried. Will you wait here for me, please?"

K8 grabbed his arm. "Wait, ain't that your mate?" Ian followed her gaze to the stage and stared in disbelief. For there, on the stage, in a severe state of drunkenness, was Dave. The lead singer of The Syphilitic Corpses spoke into the microphone. "Now, listen here, you cunts. My mate Dave here wants to sing a special song for a special girl. He says he's in love with her, but I reckon he just wants to bone her brains out. Over to you, Dave."

Dave stood in front of the microphone, eyes wide, trying to focus through the drunken blurriness. He spread his feet wider to keep his balance. He nodded to the band.

"I don't want to bone her brains out!" Dave whined back at the singer, forgetting that he was in receiving distance of the microphone.

Someone shouted 'poof!'

"Not on Saturdays." Dave snapped at whoever had questioned his sexuality, the drummer of the band backed him up with a badly timed ba-dum-tss. "This song is dedicated to Barbarella The Barmaid. I shall do this every week until I win your heart." Cries of *sad wanker* and *creepy fucker* came from the milling crowd. The song that had begun was a Black Sabbath number, a quiet, trippy song called "Planet Caravan."

Ian couldn't bear to watch, hiding his face against K8's left shoulder. Not only was Dave going to make a complete arse of himself, but he'd never pull Barbarella now.

Dave closed his eyes and started singing. "*We sailed, through endless skies, stars shine like eyes. The black night sighs...*" The crowd seemed to like it and started swaying in time.

"He isn't doing a bad job," K8 said. Ian plucked up the courage to look in his mate's direction.

Dave felt really, really, mind-blowingly pissed. He was on stage in *The Troff* singing in front of everyone in there; the only thing was, he wasn't entirely certain whether or not he was actually awake. Words were still coming out of his mouth, most of them intelligible.

He opened his left eye; about sixty faces looked at him from the dancefloor.

He closed it again.

It was at the start of the third verse that he felt that hot acidy feeling in his stomach. The bile was rising. *I must make it! Only five more sentences left. "Bathed in cool breeze, silver starlight, breaks down from night."*

Only three lines left. The bile was four feet high and rising.

"*And so we pass on by, the crimson eye, of great god Mars...*" He could feel it burning at the back of his throat. *Come on*, he pushed himself, only five more words left. "*As we travel the...*" The vomit exploded in a massive torrent of brown. Had Dave opened his eyes, he may have been able to direct his geyser of gastric gruel away from the rather large Hell's Angel type. But, unfortunately, this was not the case. The rather large Hell's Angel type was saturated in Dave's puke.

# Chapter 5: Sabbath Stones and Broken Bones

Ian saw most of what happened but he wasn't sure whether Dave had fallen into the crowd or whether he had been pulled into it. "Oh fuck," He cursed. "I'm going to have to go and help him." Ian shot K8 a worried look.

"I'll wait for you outside," she said and gave him a full-on snog. "Be careful, if you have to fight, fight dirty, kick him in the bollocks, and leg it."

Ian ventured into the crowd. He could hear Dave before he could see him. As Ian got closer to the stage, he could see a massive, hairy bastard of a man kicking the shite out of an unconscious Dave. Although the Hell's Angel guy was considerably bigger than Ian, it didn't stop him lunging at him and screaming, "Oi you cunt!" Ian jumped on the Hell's Angel bloke's back (the bloke's name was Norman, by the way, which is what I am henceforth going to call him. Something I should have done earlier, probably), grabbing him around the neck. Norman swung Ian around and threw him against the stage. Ian hit the stage, rolled off, and fell to the floor. Norman was bent over Dave, shouting at him to get up. Dave's face was covered in blood from a split lip and bloody nose. He opened his eyes groggily.

Norman smiled. "That's better." He raised his fist, ready to smash it down again, when Dave's left hand shot up, grabbed a handful of his huge beard, and tugged downwards. In Dave's right hand he held a lighter. Guess the consequences.

The crowd parted like the Red Sea at the horrific sight of a monstrous Hell's Angel with a beard of fire.

Norman ran into the toilets, slipped in some piss on the floor, and fell head-first into the toilet bowl. The flush mechanism had given up the ghost forty-three minutes earlier so the toilet water wasn't exactly Evian. It was the end of a bad night for Norman. His beard had taken six years to grow and now it was reduced to a little more than a few inches of fluff, singed and riddled with puke, piss and shit.

He wasn't even a Hell's Angel; he didn't even own a motorcycle. He drove a three-wheeled Reliant Robin.

It was his pride and joy: jet-black with orange-and-red flames licking up the sides. He called it *The Beast.*

As Norman stared at his reflection in the cracked, filthy mirror beside the rusted condom machine, he knew he would not be able to rest until he had his revenge on that little motherfucker. That little motherfucker who had thrown up on him. That little motherfucker who had thrown up on him and burnt his beard off.

Ian helped Dave up and they hobbled off towards the exit. The cold air of the early morning hit them as soon as they got outside.

"Do you reckon he'll come after us?"

Ian shrugged. "I don't know. I hope not. He's a regular, though, always sits in there on his own. Dresses like a Hell's Angel, but he isn't. I wouldn't have thought he'd try owt again. If he does, we'll just have to stick together, or tell the fucking police."

Ian craned his neck and looked around. "Shit, you reckon he's still out here?" Asked Dave.

No sign of the burnt biker, but there was K8, standing outside the chippy, clutching three white paper parcels.

"Oh, for fuck's sake, now is not the time for perving," said Dave.

K8 smiled and walked towards them. What the fuck does she want? Thought Dave. *Maybe she saw the fight and wants to give me some sympathy*. She leant forward and gave Ian a long, lingering kiss. Dave's face was a picture.

"Dave, mate," Ian smirked, "This is K8. We sort of got it on tonight."

"K8, this is Dave," Ian said. K8 smiled and handed them each a white paper parcel and kept one for herself. "Here you go, fellas; I got you some medicinal chips; nothing like a bit of grease to conquer the effects of violence and alcohol. I hope you're both okay?"

Ian looked his mate up and down. "I think we'll be okay, just a few minor cuts and bruises. Shall we go to yours, mate?"

Dave awoke from his gobsmacked trance, "Yeah, okay."

Ian turned to K8."Is that okay with you? You can sleep in the spare room and I'll sleep on the sofa or something, or I'll call you a taxi?"

K8 nodded. "Okay, lead the way, gentlemen."

The trio climbed up the hill that led to the block of flats where Dave lived. Lots of thoughts were swishing around in his head amongst the alcoholic swamp. Like the fact that there would be no more blokey nights out – Ian would be sure to bring that hot little number with him. He would have to stop saying things like 'babe', 'slut', 'bitch', 'whore' and 'hot little number' whilst she was around. They wouldn't be able to have in-depth gross-out competitions where they tried to put each other off sex. The only thing that had come close to dampening the Eternal flame that was Dave's libido was the time he was eating takeaway korma and Ian said the immortal line, 'she's so fucking hot I'd eat curry out of her arse hole.' He had actually gagged and Ian finished his curry and chalked it up to one of his greatest achievements.

*Shit, man*. Blokes acted differently when they got girls. They expected their mates to act differently around their girls. Have manners for fuck's sake. That was if Ian still wanted to hang around with him at all! They might want to do coupley things like going to the cinema, shopping, going out for meals, looking at mortgages, having sex. Dave shuddered.

In a way, it made him all the more determined to woo Barbarella. He would go down the pub tomorrow night and serenade her with another of Ozzy's classics.

As he followed them up the hill, he studied K8's shapely arse, hypnotised by its rhythmic movement, and wondered what the chances would be of getting to see her naked. They could pretend it was an accident.

He embraced the chippy parcel like one would cradle a baby in a blanket and erased such thoughts from his mind. Ian would burn his face and God only knew what evil K8 was capable of. Well, they both saw her lay that bloke out that time and no matter how fucking hot it looked from where they were, adhered to the pub windows by their own saliva, he was almost certain being the receptacle of her knuckles wouldn't be such a turn on. Despite Ian screaming behind the soundproofed glass, 'I want to die beneath your fists!'

Dave sighed, he'd just have to take the lock off the bathroom door and hope for the best.

Dave announced that he had a full bottle of vodka in the fridge (Tesco's own brand) and that it needed drinking.

"What have you got to mix it with?" K8 asked, setting down her chips on the kitchen table.

Dave opened the fridge. "Umm, milk, lager, Marmite, cooking oil, or Coke?"

K8 pondered for a second. "Think I'll choose Coke, please."

Dave grabbed a plastic pint glass and poured vodka and Coke. "Ian?"

"Coke, please. I don't think it'll go with the others, especially milk." Ian ripped open his chippy parcel and started greedily stuffing his face with chips before remembering he was with a lady.

Dave handed Ian his drink and put some vodka in a glass for himself. "Think I'll try the milk."

K8 made a disgusted face. "No, don't! It'll be foul!"

"Yeah, mate—it'll curdle," said Ian.

Regardless of his companions' advice, Dave mixed his vodka with milk and knocked it back. "It's not that bad, actually," he said, before legging it to the window. He stuck his head out and regurgitated the vodka-and-milk combo. After wiping his mouth on his sleeve, wincing at his cut lip, he said, "You should definitely try it. Like alcoholic scrambled eggs. Think the milk was off."

Just at that moment, eleven storeys down, a sad Hell's Angel wannabe was walking past, fiddling with the singed remnants of his beard, freezing cold from having to wash in a pub sink. The vomit that rained down on him was still warm when it hit him. He seriously considered buying a sombrero.

# Chapter 6: Paint the Loo Bowl with a Rainbow

When Dave awoke, he had all the tell-tale signs of the morning after. The morning after a night's heavy drinking. The first sign: it didn't feel as if he'd even been to sleep. It was as if he'd blinked and it had gone from night to day in the matter of a millisecond. Second sign: his tongue felt as dry as a doormat. The taste in his mouth was a cocktail of alcohol and sick, with a hint of chip. He felt sore all over; his lip stung where it had split. He couldn't detect a headache, but he had experienced this before.

Your body lulls you into a false sense of security. You think you've gotten off lightly after binge drinking: yeah, you ache all over, but you can put up with that. But headaches, you really hate and you're so relieved that you haven't got one. Then you sit up.

Your head feels as though it's being slowly crushed by an American wrestler who weighs like four-hundred-and-thirty-two pounds [it has to be in pounds because it sounds heavier]. The headache activates the nausea button in your stomach and it's paint-the-loo-bowl-with-a-rainbow time.

Dave wiped his mouth on some loo roll and flushed the toilet. He knew he wouldn't go back to bed even though he felt like death warmed up. He was always better off walking around, or outside in the fresh air.

He staggered towards the bathroom and was just about to go in when he stopped suddenly. Standing in front of the sink was K8 in a tiny black vest top and black knickers. *Jesus Christ,* he thought, taking in every detail, *Ian's a very lucky man.*

"'s okay, I'm coming out now," she said, seeing Dave's reflection.

What the fuck is she doing running around the joint with hardly any clothes on and leaving the door open?!

"Hey, you're alright, I don't mind watching... I mean, *waiting*!" Dave said, trying to stand in a way that best concealed his rapidly approaching erection.

K8 chuckled and finished wiping off the previous night's make-up. She added to his torture by using both hands to put her hair in a scrunchie her breasts heaving upwards. "There. I'm done."

Dave moved out of her way and she disappeared into the spare bedroom. *The dirty bitch,* he thought, *sleeping with Ian when they've only just met! The lucky bastard!* Dave shut the bathroom door behind him and filled the sink with cold water.

He dunked his face in and left it there for a few seconds. It felt wonderful; revitalising. When he stood up he could hear noises coming from the spare bedroom. Sex noises! Passionate moanings and groanings.

*Oh, for fuck's sake,* Dave said under his breath, *you don't make fuck noises like that if there's someone else in the flat with you, it's supposed to be a private, special matter of extreme intimacy between two consenting adults.* Actually, it didn't bother him, he was just jealous.

After seeing K8 in her underwear, he was still remarkably turned on, and he needed to relieve the pressure, visions of naked Barbarella in the bathroom beside him flashed behind his eyelids.

Just as he came into the sink, his mobile phone started ringing from the other room. He pulled the plug out and made himself more decent. He heard Ian answer his phone. *It didn't take him long*, he mused.

"Hello, Mrs. Smith," Ian said. "Oh, okay. I'm sorry, Stella."

He unlocked the door and went into the living room to find Ian sat with Dave's phone to his ear.

"Oh, I'm fine, thank you Stella...yeah, David is fine. No, he hasn't found a girlfriend yet." Ian chuckled sweetly. "Oh, yes, I met a girl last night... Her name is K8. Yes, I'll do my best to try and find someone for David. He has his eye on someone. No, he's not homosexual."

Dave snatched the phone off Ian, who sat laughing silently. "You silly fucker, do you think I fell for that? I'm not a complete and utter tit-head, you know!"

Ian looked horrified and pointed at the phone.

"Oh fuck," was all Dave could say for a few seconds. "Umm... hello, Mum?"

"Hello dear," came the voice from the phone. "I tried to call you yesterday but I got through to a wrong number, I think. Whoever it was was a foul-mouthed young blighter, too."

Dave grimaced; obviously, he had traumatised his mother so much that she refused to believe yesterday's episode. "Oh well, these things happen."

"Yes, they do, can't trust these cordless phones. How are you? I hope you've had a haircut, when you sent those photos in the summer, your hair was getting a bit long."

Dave twiddled his blond locks. "Yes, it's sensible now. I've got the same style as Ian."

"Oh, he's such a nice young man. You must bring him over to stay."

After several minutes of listening to apparently amusing incidents and anecdotes from the dinner parties of his parents, his mum finally said goodbye and told him to study hard. Dave slumped down onto the sofa. "How the hell am I going to tell my parents I'm not at Uni?"

*

Norman stared at his reflection in the cheap white bathroom cabinet. His once-beloved beard, his former pride and his joy, had been reduced to stubble. It used to reach down to his stomach. Big and black, it was. This was the first time he'd seen his neck in four years.

Norman was a large man. He had a scraggly mess of long black hair, a gigantic beer belly, and piercings in both ears. He stood at around six-foot-seven and was covered in tattoos. Skulls, snakes and daggers sprang out from his arms and chest.

Norman walked out of the bathroom and into a small living-room. More skulls and snakes decorated the walls and the furniture by way of posters and gothic ornaments. He picked up a black T-shirt off the floor and stuck his head through it, pulling it down over his yellow-stained vest. He hitched up his filthy Levi's and picked up a denim jacket with the sleeves ripped off. Norman knew exactly where the little shit would be. *The Troff*. He would go down there again and again until he had pulverised him. Or at least do the same to him. Burn, pull or shave off all his hair and rip out his piercings. That's what he wanted to do. But enough about that for today.

Today, Norman was on a quest. For years, he had wanted to become a Hell's Angel. It had always been his dream. He had been trying to get into the Walsall chapter, The Wasters, for the last year-and-a-half. A couple of the guys, Squizz and Nosher, had become quite fond friends of his. They were always going on at him about the things they'd do when he got into the Angels. The only reason he couldn't get in was due to the leader of this particular sect; a massive hulk of a man who called himself Reaper. He was toying with Norman. He kept telling him that he had to prove himself worthy of membership. Secretly, the whole gang were laughing at him. They had him doing no end of stupid things to prove himself worthy.

This time, Norman was due to meet Reaper, Squizz and Nosher at a pub in Birmingham.

As he got into his three-wheeler, a wave of sadness swept over him. This could be one of the last times—or the last time— he drove *The Beast*. Reaper had promised him that if he were to do this task successfully, he would become a fully-fledged member of The Wasters. He had even shown Norman his member's jacket: sleeveless denim with a green skull on the back, complete with red eyes and black teeth. Above the skull in black letters were the words, "The Wasters", and beneath was Norman's Angel name, "Viper."

One of the guys knew someone who had a decent motorbike to sell, and who would sell it to Norman for a discount price. So he would have to sell *The Beast*.

Norman shut The Beast's door and walked into the pub, a mixture of feelings running through him. He didn't care what they wanted him to do; whatever the task was, he was up for it. He would succeed.

Thirty-five minutes later Norman left the pub looking slightly dejected. One reason for this was due to the fact that he was completely naked apart from his Doc Martens. He covered his genitals with one hand and held a pint of Guinness in the other. His mission, to get from the pub in Birmingham to the Troff in Walsall by precisely ten of the clock. He wasn't allowed to use his car, and furthermore, he was not allowed to spill or drink the pint.

He was glad it was dark, but unhappy about everything else. There he was, stuck behind a pub in the second biggest city in the UK, stark bollock naked. How in the name of Krishna would he be able to get back to Walsall in two hours without being arrested? Reaper said he didn't care how he did it, as long as he didn't use his car and as long as the pint glass and contents remained intact. Also, he was given permission to acquire new clothing. How the hell am I supposed to do that?

He aimed to get to the railway station somehow and hide out in the toilets on the train back to Walsall. He knew there would be no chance of shoplifting any clothes, not just because of the shops being shut but because of the snowball in hell's chance of blending in with the other shoppers. No one would miss a hairy, naked bloke of epic proportions.

He glanced down at his watch. 8:15 pm. Knowing he had better make a move, he looked around trying to decide what would be his first. Just then, he saw it—a quick way of getting from the pub to the station. Propped up against one of the fire exits was a bike. An old and rusty bike, but it looked as though it might work. *Right,* he thought, *I've got transport.* But how the fuck was he supposed to ride a bike and not spill the stout? Norman cheered as he spotted a plastic bottle, half-filled with what he suspected was *not* apple juice. He carefully placed the pint down and unscrewed the lid. *Yep – piss.* He poured the stuff down a drain and was just about to pour the stout into the bottle when he changed his mind. Visions of it spilling everywhere went through his head.

Norman took a large mouthful of Guinness, careful not to swallow, and pressed his pursed lips against the pissy opening. As he spat the black liquid into the stinking bottle, he tried to not picture the cheesy, encrusted knob of some tramp oozing out his chlamydia juices. He failed.

Somehow, he managed to convert the whole pint into the bottle. He screwed the lid on firmly, plonked the bottle inside the empty glass, and tried to make himself comfortable on the bike. He wished it had a seat.

## Chapter 7: Trains, Pains, and Tank Girl

Unfortunately for Norman, the city centre was relatively busy. Many surprised bystanders were silenced mid-sentence, stopped in their tracks at the sight of an enormous hairy man on a mountain bike hurtling down the high street. An enormous hairy *naked* man on a rusty mountain bike with no seat, sagging arse poised just centimetres over what could very well be penetrative death, hurtling at high-speed, down the high street.

Out from the alley he went, and over a road, narrowly avoiding being clipped by a double-decker bus. Screaming and screaming all the way, "Get out of the fucking way!" as he sped through the many, many people.

*So far, so good,* thought Norman, as he cycled down the high street. *The most people are doing is staring in disbelief.* None were reaching for their mobile phones yet. He raced around a corner at break-neck speed, knocking a Big Issue seller to the floor in the process. The quickest way to the station was through the shopping centre.

As he turned to go down the road towards the station, he could just make out the yellow of a police car up ahead. "Oh fuck," he cried. Taking a slight detour, he turned and headed towards a different shopping centre. It would take longer, but he would still be able to reach his destination.

Norman took the road beside the shopping centre. The only problem was, it was the main road, so he had to dodge and swerve past the oncoming vehicles.

Norman brought the bike up onto the path and started to pedal faster. The station was in sight, only about a hundred yards away. He was going to make it! Then, SMASH!

Norman lay on the pavement wondering what in the name of Jehovah had happened, pain searing through his skull. Checking that the bottle and glass were still intact, he sighed with relief. Looking up, he saw a telephone box, wide open, the bike's handlebars sticking through the shattered glass of the door. A man stood before him, distraught and confused (it's not every day a naked man bikes into the phone box you're using). Norman started to laugh, for the man was dressed as Father Christmas! It was fucking September. He stood up, towering over the man. "Now, we can do this the easy way, or we can do this the hard way."

*

K8, Ian and Dave had been in the flat most of the day. A short visit to the nearest supermarket—not Tesco—to get food and booze was their only trip out. They had been drinking for three hours before it was time for them to venture out.

The three of them slouched on the sofa, staring at the closing credits of a film.

"The thing about Tank Girl, though," Dave started, "is that she is just so fucking hot! I mean, I know there's been some global disaster or such, that's why water is like gold dust, but how can she still manage to look so hot?"

Ian stroked his chin in thought. "I like to believe she has a secret supply of beer somewhere that she has to drink to survive."

Dave's eyes lit up. "Maybe she washes in it?"

"Yeah!" Chuckled Ian.

"Hey, maybe afterwards, after she's washed all her nooks and crannies out, she re-bottles the beer," Dave said, almost dream-like.

K8 sat forward, gobsmacked. "Oh, for fuck's sake. Gentlemen, has it escaped your attention that there is a lady present? And that I, as a lady, might find your talk of drinking Tank Girl's body-filth beer repulsive?"

Dave and Ian both hung their heads like two naughty schoolboys. "Sorry."

K8 smirked. "Actually, I don't find it repulsive, but that's not the point. How would you feel if I said I wanted to eat Johnny Depp's sweaty Y-fronts?"

"I'd ask, 'would you like fries with that?'" Said Ian.

K8 laughed, slapped both men on their thighs and said, "Right, are we going down to the pub and get this girl, or what?"

"Okay, okay," Dave said, leaping up. "How do I look?" He patted down some wayward strands of hair and brushed remnants of sour cream and onion Pringles from his t-shirt. Dressed in scruffy jeans and a tight black t-shirt with, "Necrophilia, rigour mortis makes me hard!" he was quite a picture.

"She'll not be able to resist you, mate," said K8.

"Yeah," said Ian, "if she doesn't fall for you tonight, then she's got to be a lesbian."

Filthy, perverse, sexually explicit images sped through Dave's mind. "Hmm ... now there's a thought."

K8 got up and walked to the door, "Come on, cease this banter; for we must leave this lofty retreat for pastures new."

"Art thou certain, fair maiden?" Said Ian, bowing. "Wouldst thou rather force Sir David to venture out into the bleak evening tide alone and let I, your servant, your bold knight, impale you on my lengthy lance?"

Dave looked at the pair of them. "What the holy flying arse-chip are you going on about? Jesus wept! Come on, let's move!"

"So," K8 began, pointing her finger like a conductor's baton as she walked backwards in front of the two goons. "Now, please don't take this the wrong way-"

"Oh, I'm totally going to take it the wrong way now," Dave whined.

"Shut the fuck up and listen, wanksandwich," Ian said shooting an elbow into his ribs.

"Thank you, dear heart," K8 blew a kiss to Ian and continued talking to Dave. "Now, Mr. Masturbation Burrito, I know how in the olden days these gestures were seen as romantic, you know, flowers, chocolates and serenading below balconies, but The Barmaid-"

"Barberella."

"That's right, how the hell could I forget, Barberella, is a modern girl and kicks blokes arses out of the frigging Trough every weekend night. She's probably got bigger balls than you."

"I'd still love her even if she did have balls," Dave said staring off into space.

"Yeah, okay. Good. Well, what I'm getting at is, why don't you actually speak to her, tell her how you feel rather than..." K8's voice petered off into something inaudible.

"Sorry? What was that last bit?"

K8 looked at Ian who beamed back a huge, shit-eating grin. "You're on your own, babe."

K8 sighed, "rather than being a creepy pervert. There, I said it."

Dave staggered to a halt clutching at the imaginary arrow that pierced his heart. "Ow."

Ian patted him on the back. "She has a point, mate."

"You would say that she's your girlfriend. You love her points." Dave let out a filthy drain laugh at an unintentional innuendo. 'Her points.' *God, I'm hilarious without even trying*. When he realised neither Ian nor K8 had either heard or understood his brilliant joke he decided to compromise. "Look, we all know that I am a gutless coward…"

"It's true."

"Thank you, Ian. And the only way I can muster up enough bravado to even talk to the Trough bikes-"

"The what?" K8 stopped abruptly, hands on hips.

"Oh, it's cool," Dave began, "it's what we call the really doggish bints that'll pretty much do anything for a pint and a packet of scratchings."

"And you think it's okay to call these girls that? They have feelings too, you know?"

Dave snorted, "No they don't, once I got off with this one girl called Emma and I'd been going at it for five minutes and she asked if it was in yet. And this other time-"

"Dave shut the fuck up!" Ian clamped both hands around Dave's mouth whilst he still had some teeth left.

He raised his palms up in defeat and was released. "Okay, that was disrespectful towards women. I'm sorry." Dave looked at Ian doubtful, "Maybe I should just stay single and wank? If I've got to watch what I say all the time…"

"Look," K8 sighed, "we know there's more to you than just being a daft, pervy twat-"

"There is?" Dave appeared delighted.

"Yeah, just don't ask us to list 'em for fuck's sake," Ian muttered.

"Sure," K8 said, not even convincing herself, "but you need to show Barberella the real you. Show her what makes you stand out from the rest of the men."

Dave turned to Ian, "do you think I should show her that thing I can do with my-"

"No!"

"No," K8 agreed, "whatever the hell that is if it can make Ian make that face then save it for another day, a long way away. Just get in there and talk to her. Be a man. Be brave. Be bold. Be a warrior, Dave."

*Be a warrior, Dave.* He liked the sound of that. But he'd need to be an incredibly, blind fucking drunk warrior first though.

The tunnel vision was back. It always happened when he first saw her each time. Everything aside from her existed in a swirl of black and brown and scattered streaks of yellow. He was a rabbit ensnared by the headlights of a speeding juggernaut. Nothing worked for a few seconds. Standing was possible but full facial atrophy made him look like a slathering loon. At the end of this imaginary tunnel was the only thing he could focus on. The goddess of his innermost desires—Barbarella!

Tonight, she looked even more bewitching. A tight black-and-purple bodice, which made him almost die, and a black mini-skirt and fishnets, not to mention sixteen-hole Dr Martens. She flashed her hauntingly beautiful eyes in Dave's direction, the black eye shadow and mascara only emphasising them more. And again, his head-jukebox selected his Black Sabbath album and turned the volume up to eleven. He felt a hand on his shoulder, and K8 asked him what he wanted to drink.

"Flerpnerper," Dave said, more noise than actual language.

"Just get him a Newkie, babe," Ian said, "He's always like this for the first few minutes. I've never seen anything like it."

*

A green-and-yellow train came to a hissing halt on platform one at Walsall railway station. The doors slid open and half-a-dozen people got off the train. One, in particular, was a bearded bulk of a man in a Santa costume that was way too small for him.

Norman checked out the clock; it was twenty-past nine. It would take him ten minutes to get to the pub. He poured the stout from the lemonade bottle into the glass and continued walking towards The Trough, a triumphant look on his face.

*

Six pints later, Dave was on stage, beaming with confidence. He had sensibly chosen to ignore K8's advice. Talking was for girls. In the middle of a five-minute guitar solo, he took the mic. "Today, I watched Tank Girl, and I'd like to do an inspired act for Barbarella."

"What the fuck's he doing? He said he was going to behave and talk to her," K8 asked Ian as they stood in the crowd, watching in horror. Dave pulled out a pair of scissors from his pocket. They looked very sharp.

"One thing you'll learn about Dave is, that he's a fucking idiot."

To a drum roll, Dave plucked at his t-shirt and cut a chunk of it away. A few whistles and hollers erupted from the dancefloor. He threw the piece into the crowd. A wide gash revealed his white belly. Another drum roll and another slice was snipped away.

*

Norman walked through the beer garden. The youngsters puffing weed casually eyed his Santa costume as he entered the back of the pub. The flat pint of Guinness felt like the Olympic torch. None of that poncy modern day shit either. Old Greek shit. He felt as though he had battled fucking monsters for these cunts and this was his triumphant moment. He could see Reaper, Squizz and Nosher on the dance floor watching some shite band on the stage.

Sudden silence in the audience. Dave stared, pale-faced. He slowly looked down at his opened hand. Lying in his blood-covered hand was his left nipple. "Oh, fucking *fuck*!"

Ian said something along those lines too—as did K8. Dave jumped off the stage and ran towards the toilets, the others following behind him. "Don't throw it out," shouted Ian. "They might be able to sew it back on!"

Dave ran down the corridor towards the toilet, colliding with a guy in a Father Christmas costume and spilling his pint all over him in the process.

# Chapter 8: Surprise! More Sex and Violence!

So close. Norman couldn't believe it. He had been ten feet away from Reaper, Squizz and Nosher. He looked at them hopefully and watched Reaper shake his gigantic head. Filled with rage, Norman threw the glass against the wall and slammed open the toilet door, hell-bent on killing the little motherfucker who had jeopardized his lifelong dream.

Ian sprang into action. "Go to the bar and get the ice bucket and some towels or something, and meet us outside in five." He kissed K8 on the forehead and ran into the bathroom, screaming.

Dave was in a heap on the floor, battered and bloodied. Chunks of hair had been ripped from his scalp. Norman was delivering kick after kick to his stomach.

Ian threw all his weight against the big lug, sending them both crunching into the wall. Ian didn't waste any time and punched Norman in the face as hard as he could. The force caused the guy's head to strike the condom machine and he fell to his knees.

Ian grabbed his friend's legs and quickly dragged him into the corridor. Norman came stumbling out behind them, the porcelain lid of the toilet cistern in his hands. He swung it hard into Ian's stomach. The blow winded Ian and he fell to the floor, catching his head on one of the metal bar stools on the way down. Norman raised the lid high above Dave's head, a look of pure hatred in his eyes.

Then, like a scene from a movie, he fell to his knees, then onto his back, unconscious. Standing behind him, looking like an *even* sexier version of *Xena, Warrior Princess*, was Barbarella, a hefty-looking beige fire extinguisher in her hands. She blew a strand of blue hair away from her face, bent down, and yelled right into Norman's face, "Leave him alone, you bastard!"

*

Barbarella needed a drink. Due to that night's events, the pub had closed ninety minutes early, which was really shit for business. She waited till the police had gone and the ambulance had taken the blokes away. She had an inkling what had been going on but never had the pub seen so much violence. A couple of her mates had come back home with her to help her overcome her ordeal (and get pissed). She could've killed that bloke, if she'd hit him any harder— she was surprised they didn't arrest her. For some reason, though, they were satisfied with a statement. Although if he decided to press charges her life could be over.

*

The two ambulances drove towards the hospital; luckily, none of their patients were that critical.

*

Norman came round after a couple of minutes, convinced he'd split his head open and his brains were spilling out. This wasn't too far from the truth.

He had been fortunate to get away with a slight concussion and a massive cut on his head that would definitely need stitches. He hurt all over, especially his nose and jaw, and his right index finger was bandaged, with blood seeping through the dressing. Norman would find out later that during the fight he had somehow managed to rip off the nail.

*

Barbarella found porn videos really annoying. She loved watching them, but purely for comedy value. A couple of her mates had brought a really dodgy looking one around. She and her mates, Ange and Lise, thought there was nothing more enjoyable than watching porn and getting drunk (to be fair, they're not wrong).

The video in question was entitled, "The Life Erotic," and it was in German with English subtitles. It was pretty basic by the looks of the cover: just a boring man and woman.

Barbarella sat on the sofa, remote control in hand. To her left sat Ange, who looked like a gothic human incarnation of the cartoon character, *Daria*. She wore black-rimmed glasses and had short sensible black hair with a solitary streak of red in it that could be taken out for work.

Lise was baby-faced and big with blood-red hair, piercings, and a killer smile.

In front of the three was a coffee table covered in no end of random shit. A semi-circle had been carved into the mountain of trash to make way for a full bottle of Southern Comfort and three glasses.

Barbarella pressed play and said, "Right, are you ready for some hot, hard, German action?"

"C' mon, bring on the bratwurst," cheered Ange.

*

In the second ambulance, Ian was sitting beside Dave, face in hands. He didn't know what the hell he'd do if anything happened to Dave. The daft, stupid, idiotic, wanker. He loved him like a brother; it hurt to see him in such a state—unlucky, unaware, unconscious.

They wanted to x-ray Ian as they suspected the blow from the cistern lid might have cracked a rib—but he doubted it. He would've gone anyway, after making sure K8 got in a taxi he climbed in the ambulance and went with Dave.

Ian discreetly wiped away a tear before it had a chance to continue its downward trajectory. He sniffled and sighed as he took in the specifics of Dave's injuries. Those he could see, at least.

*

Some really ugly spotty guy with the obligatory seventies porn star moustache smiled at the camera and pulled out his penis. It was enormous! The girls gasped in disbelief. "They must have touched that up," said Lise disgustedly but moving closer to the television. "No one can have a cock that big. It's horrible."

Barbarella grimaced. "Girl must have a bucket fanny." She leant back, put her feet up and sipped her drink, glad to be able to relax for a bit. Physically anyway. The night's events played in her head. That daft prick getting up on the stage again and making an even bigger tit of himself than ever before. It was ironic really. He only ever spoke to her when he had that much to drink he was barely intelligible. But working in pubs for a couple of years soon made you bilingual where pissheads were concerned. She didn't think he was that bad looking, a little bit weedier than her normal type but he had very pretty eyes. When they're not fucking well staring at me like a fucking goldfish who's just shot up!

On the screen, a busty brunette appeared, got down on her knees, and spoke in German, "Lassen Sie mich es schmecken."

(The English subtitles read, "Let me taste it.") It was then that the three girls found out it was one of those subtle pornos that manage not to show anything too hard-core. The next thing they knew, the camera shot from the lady's nose upwards in one shot and closed in on the bloke's sweaty face.

He growled like the aforementioned American wrestler and said with as much emotion he could muster with his dick in the mouth of a lady, "saugen, dass schwanz, Hündin." (Which of course, means, "Suck that cock, Bitch.")

The girls were treated to another close-up of the woman's face, gazing up at the man, cheeks bulging. She made a wet sucking noise as she removed his cock from her mouth. "Ja, du magst es nicht?" ("Yes, you like it don't you?")

"Well, duh," Ange said, "what guy doesn't like his dick in a chick's gob?"

The man groaned and said, "Ja, ja."

The girls choked on their drinks when they read the next subtitles: "Setzen Sie es in mich, ich kann es nicht mehr nehmen." ("Put it inside me, I cannot take it any longer.") Then an unnecessary close-up of the swollen tip of the man's penis led to her saying the immortal line, "Oh mein Gott, was für ein riesiges Glockenende, es wird sicher nicht passen." ("Oh my God, what an enormous bell end, surely it won't fit.")

Ange roared with laughter and repeated the words, "glocke ende" but seriously doubted the linguist's translation capabilities. She was an intelligent girl and she was sure that the term *bell end* wasn't international.

*

Dave lay on the stretcher; the ambulance staff had carefully removed his t-shirt to dress some minor cuts and he was beneath a white sheet, exposed from the shoulder up. His shoulders were covered in small cuts and huge blossoming bruises that looked incredibly painful. He had a hand-shaped red mark around his neck where Norman had tried to choke him, and five sets of little red crescents where Norman's nails had drawn blood. And then there was the loss of his nipple.

*

The man lay down on the wooden floor and the woman eased herself onto his outrageous erection. After getting comfortable, she began to push herself up and down on it. The bloke growled really, really loudly, causing further bouts of laughter from his viewers. "Fahren Sie es, wie Sie es noch nie zuvor geritten haben." ("Ride it like you've never ridden it before.")

The couple were going at it harder and harder, faster and faster until the man said something that the film-makers chose not to translate, and the woman looked up at him and pleaded, "Komm über meine pendelnden Brüste, wirst du?" ("Come over my pendulous breasts, will you?") And the man withdrew his member and did as instructed. He roared like a tiger and finally his last words before The Teletubbies appeared and said, "Eh-oh," were, "Und ich werde ausgegeben." ("And I'm spent.")

Barberella had completely zoned out letting Lise and Ange's cackled and comments become background noise whilst she felt the booze take effect and thought about the silly twat that was trying to win her affection. She surfaced, dazed and confused at the sight of four multicoloured Teletubbies dancing around and chasing a balloon. "What in the name of Hare Krishna's Aunt Mavis is going on?"

"Maybe Po's gonna make Tinky-Winky his whore and bend him over that wall," suggested Lise. They both looked at Ange for an explanation. It was she who'd brought the video along.

Ange looked just as puzzled. "I swear it was fine last week; there was this great scene with a milkmaid and two guys in lederhosen. My brother must have pissed about with it."

Lise looked horrified. "Oh my god, how old's your brother? You shouldn't leave porn around; it'll warp his mind."

"It's okay—he's twenty-one, and already warped."

*

Dave was unrecognisable. His lips were swollen and bleeding, black with bruising, and there were huge plum-like bulges where his eyes should be. There was no way he'd be able to open his eyes for a few days. The piercings in his right ear had been ripped out and his earlobe was torn badly and he had also chipped four of his teeth and swallowed another. Ian stopped another tear in its track; he had no idea what they were going to do. He knew the police wouldn't be much use. They didn't do anything when his younger brother had been beaten up by some group of yobs, just because he had answered them back when they had called him a 'greebo'. They didn't even do much when the same group of yobs attacked Ian's brother and threw him off a railway bridge in time for the 7:15 from Birmingham.

*Oh, fucking hell*, thought Ian, trying not to think about stuff that happened years ago. He had met Dave shortly after, and he kind of reminded him of his brother even though there were only a couple of years between them. He hadn't told Dave about him; they never seemed to be serious enough to bring it up. It's hard to bring up something like that when everyone's always pissing about. But it was the easy way out, not to think about serious things, put them off till another day.

The ambulance pulled up at the hospital.

*

*Fuck it. Maybe a weedier guy won't be as much of a dick as the others were.* Barbarella stood up. "Sorry to do this, guys, you're welcome to crash here, use what you want, but I've got to go out. I'll explain later."

With that, she grabbed her bag and coat and ran to the door, leaving the two girls without explanation.

# Chapter 9: From the Belly of the Beast to the Arms of an Angel

The first things Dave saw when he awoke was a white ceiling and strip lighting. The first thing he felt was intense pain. He thought he must be still dreaming when he saw the angelic face of Barbarella smiling sympathetically at him. He guessed he was in the hospital, but why, he couldn't remember exactly, probably something to do with all the pain. But that didn't matter. All that mattered was that Barbarella was here, beside him, smiling, albeit sympathetically, *at him*! Lustful smiling would have been better, though. Although saying that Dave wasn't sure he'd be able to brave moving just yet, let alone perform the complete karma sutra with his angel. For some reason he didn't feel at all shy like usual, no heart beating in his throat; he even felt capable of intelligible speech. They must have pumped him full of some shit hot drugs; this was not normal.

"So, have I died and gone to Valhalla?" Dave said, almost certain that his pronunciation was completely wrong, with far too many 'h's. He also realised that it hurt to talk.

Barbarella smirked. It was a beautiful smirk. "Do I look like a Valkyrie?"

Dave shook his head, which hurt even more. "No, but you've got a great set of lungs. Cuz I've heard you shout last orders over Machine head! Nothing…" *Please stop,* Dave told his mouth, cursing his newfound ability to talk, "to do with your breasts." His eyes flicked down to her chest against his will and for once he was glad they were covered up. *Jesus, what shit have they got me on?*

"Thanks, I think. So, do you remember what happened?"

"The last thing I remember is going into the toilet with my nipple. Oh, shit." He looked down at his chest. A thick wad of gauze covered his left breast. "So, what are you doing here?"

"Well, first you ran into that big hairy twat who you vommed on the other night, and he basically kicked the shit out of you and Ian. Now you're here, and I was thinking about the stuff that went down and thought I'd come and see if you were okay."

"Do I look okay?"

"No, you look like shit. But I'm here to tell you that I'm going to give you a chance. Am I that scary? You know, why not, like, try being normal. Do the normal thing and strike up a conversation with me?"

When he laughed his whole face felt like it was tearing itself apart but he couldn't believe what she had just said.

"Preposterous notion!" He was certain that was the very first time he had ever used the word 'preposterous' in a sentence.

He grimaced with splitting lips.

"I could have done, I suppose, but one, I was too nervous, and two, I thought seeing as you are an extremely attractive barmaid, you would be getting propositioned all the time. For some reason, I found serenading you was easier. I have admired you from afar, yes. But being a hopeless romantic, it was the only way I could express my feelings." Dave lowered his eyes, feeling embarrassed. "So, how's Ian?"

"They patched him up and sent him home a few hours ago. Kept you in because of kicks to the head and chopped-off nipples. No permanent damage apart from the nipple loss. The hairy twat is in the next ward. Same as you, he had a minor head injury, no permanent damage. They've got a couple of coppers hanging about in case he kicks off again."

Dave sighed. "Well, I don't know how the hell I'm going to get out of this with that guy there. He acts like he wants me dead. I don't know what his problem is; all I did was vomit on him once and accidentally spill his drink."

"Ah," Barbarella said. "There's more to it than that. Apparently, Norman, that's his name, has always wanted to be a member of The Wasters, the bikers you see hanging around the pub, and he was doing his final task before they accepted him. That involved the drink you spilt. They rejected him. I'm afraid you shattered his dreams."

Dave closed his bruised eyes. "Oh, motherfuck. Why can't people just chill the fuck out and talk?"

Barbarella held his hand. It felt wonderfully soft and warm; she wore black nail varnish with red spiderwebs picked out on them. "Says the person who has to be whacked off his face on morphine before he can speak to me? Don't worry, we'll figure something out."

"Is that what they're giving-" *Oh my god,* Dave froze mid-question, *she said 'we.'* He also thought, *yes, yes, yes! She is mine! Muah-ha-ha!* And he briefly imagined her kissing every square inch of his love-length before his mind moved on to even more indecent acts from his encyclopaedic knowledge of all things filthy.

"Oh, yeah —this should cheer you up." Barbarella was about to bring him back to reality. "Ian said your parents are coming to see you the day after tomorrow."

Just when you think life is shit, things can always get worse.

Barbarella stood in the lift with Dave. They were travelling up to the eleventh floor. She leaned forward and subtly licked her lips. Dave noticed it all in extreme detail.

"Dave, I want our first kiss to be memorable." With that, she thrust herself at him, forcing him against the wall. Her hands grabbed his buttocks hard, pulling him against her body.

Dave squirmed not only due to the bruising but also with unbridled lust. Barbarella pushed her soft lips onto his and slowly slid her tongue into his mouth. Their tongues entwined, he licked the stud in her tongue and imagined it around his cock. The kiss was so intense he felt sure he was going to faint. *Jesus,* he thought, *if just one kiss from her has that effect on me, fucking her will probably kill me!* What a way to go, though! He hoped he could stop himself crying when she finally got naked in front of him.

The lift door opened and they walked to the front door of his flat. He fumbled in his jeans for his keys, leaning forward slightly so his trousers hung loose, disguising his erection. He unlocked the door and they went inside the flat. As soon as they got in the hallway, Dave knew something was up. Someone had been in his flat!

The first thing he noticed was missing was the colossal black bin bag of rubbish that had sat in the corner for the previous five days.

All the dirt and bits of fluff, along with all the dust, crumbs, and toenails, had been removed from every floor surface. The floors even sparkled with cleanliness. It was as if he'd walked in on some floor cleaner advert. This mystery do-gooder had removed all his heavy metal and girlie posters that had covered every space on his walls. Even the bits of Blue Tac were gone!

He walked cautiously into the living room, half-expecting to find a masked intruder in marigolds removing months of dust with a feather duster. More disturbing still, all his CDs were in alphabetical order and neatly stacked, and someone had swapped all his trashy horror novels and titty mags for a vast collection of books on grammar, thesauruses, and brick-thick dictionaries in several languages. Books on poetry, literature, leather-bound books by D.H. Lawrence, Shakespeare, T.S Eliot, no one alive now! There was even fucking Tolkien! Dave fucking hated Tolkien.

He ran into the kitchen—the clean, spotless kitchen.

"Fucking hell. Fucking, arsing, titting, hell." He held his breath, opened the fridge, and screamed in horror. The contents were usually limited to solid milk (being so far past its use-by date it was going through puberty) a few cans of beer, and mouldy cheese. Oh, and then there were the pot noodles (half-eaten), sausage rolls, half a tin of green baked beans, and ever since he could remember, something furry in the top left corner that he had never quite plucked up the courage to investigate. Not to mention the bottom shelf.

The bottom shelf was typically an impenetrable forest of fungal infestation that probably harboured new species of virus. But now it was not only spotless but filled with fresh fruit and vegetables!

There was an aubergine in there!

*What the fuck is an aubergine, anyway?* He wouldn't know what to do with an aubergine if it came with an instruction manual and a recipe book entitled 'What You Can Do With Your Aubergine.'

"What?" Dave asked the beaming Barbarella. "Who?"

She put a finger to his lips. "Shh, don't say a thing. This is all due to Ian and K8. I introduced myself whilst you were in the hospital. They knew you would be shitting yourself about your folks coming so they had a bit of a tidy."

That was the understatement of the century. He noticed a cringeworthy photo of his parents on the fridge. "But what about all those books? Where the fuck did they come from?"

"Ian said he's got a mate who works on a mobile library thing."

"Oh, yeah—that twat, Slimer."

"Let's just hope your parents don't notice they're all library books."

"Oh my god. I'm going to have to smarten up, cut my hair. I can't."

"I've thought about that," Barbarella said as she disappeared into the spare bedroom. She came back with a long wig the same colour as Dave's hair. "Put this on and I'll give you a haircut."

# Chapter 10: Beat the Parents

Dave looked in the full-length mirror. He was not happy with his makeover. The clean, white trainers, brown corduroy trousers and white t-shirt adorned with *Jesus is Just Alright With Me,* was just not alright with him. After much arguing, Barbarella found a cream short-sleeved shirt to go over and hide the t-shirt. Thank God she had a brother who wasn't into metal. Dave hated Barbarella's brother's clothes but not half as much as his own hair. He was grateful it was only a wig. Short and blond with a side parting, he was dressed for Bible study. His parents would see through it in a heartbeat, even with his piercings removed and facial hair trimmed.

*

"A pox on these silly contraptions," Cursed Bob the bald-headed vicar and father of Dave.

"Be patient, Bob," said his patient wife. "There's only the one lift and there are twelve floors, you know. What do you expect?"

Bob sighed, "I don't know. I suppose it's okay for a block of flats. We've not seen any graffiti and, so far, no litter."

They stared at the red numbers above the door. It went from eleven to ten. At least it was coming down.

*

There was a knock at the door. Dave reluctantly opened it. He wished Barbarella had stayed; they'd spent hardly any time together. Well, not the sort of time Dave had wanted to spend with her.

He burst into laughter at the sight of Ian before him. It was like staring at a clone of himself (only a bigger, darker-haired version.) Ian, too, had gone for the smart young man look, apart from his hair, which he had scraped back into a neat ponytail.

"Oh my god!" Was all Dave could say at first. "I can't believe you've done all this for me!"

He flung his arms around his friend just as the lift doors opened behind him and said, "I fucking love you, you old cunt." Dave looked up at his parents' disgusted faces. "Hi, Mum. Hi, Dad."

Dave had to explain his bruises. He fobbed his parents off with a lame excuse about how he fell down the treacherous steps that led up to St Matthew's church on the hill.

"And you say it's for the amateur dramatics group of the university?" Asked Stella, leaning forward in her armchair, mug of tea in hand.

Ian sat opposite Dave's mother and smiled sweetly. "Yes, that's correct. You see… David and I sort of run the group for a few hours twice a week in the evenings. We were just rehearsing a scene in our new play 'The Light came on.'" He offered a plate of chocolate digestives to Stella.

Bob smiled. "What did you say it was about?"

*Oh, for fuck's sake*, thought Dave, what the hell had Ian said? "Umm, well, it's kind of about this poor young unfortunate who has turned to drink, drugs and violence after a traumatic experience —and obviously, what you witnessed was one of the earlier scenes where he is..." Dave paused, thinking. "Thanking his brother for his birthday party."

Bob sipped his tea. "And you think the use of unsavoury language is required?"

*Big fat cancerous testicles,* Dave screamed inside his head; the last thing he wanted was a detailed conversation with his parents. "Well, one has to portray the character in his true form. It only adds to emphasise the change in him when he turns to religion."

Stella smiled at this. "And what makes him turn to religion?"

*Shitting, shitting arses*, thought Dave. *Fuck, tits, and wank.* What the fuck was he going to do? He couldn't think of any more shite. The shite well had run dry.

"Well," Began Ian. Ian to the rescue. The mighty Ian Maiden. What a guy. "Interestingly enough, Stella, the character has a near-death experience involving his own drug abuse. He wonders why he didn't die when he should have, and he cleans himself up and picks up the Bible —and then there's no stopping him."

Stella and Bob smiled at each other for a few seconds. Then Stella asked, "And what is it you're studying, Ian?"

*Oh fuck*, thought Dave.

Ian said the first subject that came into his head. "Medicine."

Bob looked straight at him. "I didn't think you could study Medicine at Birmingham University?"

*Oh fuck*, thought Ian. *Come on, blag your way out of this.*

Dave spoke up. "Oh yeah, you can now, they've changed a part of the old science block to accommodate it."

"Ah I see," said Bob.

Everything was going okay until Dave realised he must have untapped telekinetic powers. Probably the sort that pre-teen girls get when they're going through puberty and conjure up poltergeist activity, it would never be anything *Carrie* cool with his luck.

All he did was look at his parents' wedding portrait above the television. Ian had hung it there after finding it in the back of Dave's wardrobe still in the packaging.

Maybe it was telekinesis, maybe not, but when Dave looked at it, it fell off the wall and onto the floor, smashing the glass. The shock of it falling off the wall was okay; accidents happen. But it had been covering up three red sixes he had painted on the wall whilst pissed.

He and Ian had been drinking, obviously, and listening to some really hardcore Scandinavian black metal and they decided to perform a satanic ritual after thinking about Swedish women a bit too long.

This basically involved them drawing what they thought were occult symbols on the link, throwing some gone-off ham and the dead pigeon that had been on Dave's balcony for three weeks amidst it and pissing on it.

They were going to cut themselves but they realised that would hurt so they figured urine was the next best thing.

The only thing the ritual succeeded in doing was getting Dave more complaints from the Man Downstairs (not Satan, the man who lives in the flat below, his name's Peter and he's partially deaf)

In one last bid to bring The Devil through into this world, Dave scrawled a pact below the triple sixes as he had read all about how Satan loved pacts.

Aside from the buffet of dead pigeon, dodgy meat and piss Beelzebub wouldn't come visiting without there being something else in it for him as he was famous for being a selfish bastard. In exchange for the small gifts of immortality and the ability to pull anyone they wanted Dave had carved his offer in stone. Well, sharpied it on wallpaper.

Bob and Stella stared at the childlike handwriting of their son.

"I'd sell my parents to Satan for some cunt!"

After the four of them had sat in utter silence for two whole minutes and then waited for Stella to finish crying, Ian attempted to talk Dave out of the bottomless pit he was in with an elaborate story about a burglary where nothing actually got stolen.

## Chapter 11: The Mobile Library...from Hell!

*What a stroke of luck,* thought Norman. He had been sitting on a bus and saw the little fucker who had ruined his life. Outside the flats, kissing that young barmaid from the pub. Someone told him it was that bitch who'd knocked him out. They were going to get their just desserts. *An angel always gets his revenge.* As soon as he got home he would unleash The Beast, fill her up and come back here and dish it up. *A Hell's Angel never gives up.* Even though he wasn't a member of The Wasters, he was a one-man gang. Norman the lone angel. He knew exactly what he was going to do, and it involved his dad's shotgun.

As soon as Norman got home, he filled his pockets with shotgun cartridges. He took the gun from the attic, dusted it off and got to work on the barrel with his hacksaw. He didn't plan on killing anyone, just maybe shoot his kneecaps off and show his young tart what a real man was like, not some wimpy little twat. Make him cry in front of his new bird. He placed the gun beneath a dirty sack on the passenger seat of The Beast, got in and slammed the door. The engine started on the third attempt and three-wheels of raging terror roared away in a cloud of dust—and stalled at the traffic lights.

*

Dave, Barbarella, K8, and Ian were standing in the hallway when the intercom went. "Hello?"

A voice on the other end said they had a parcel for him. "Can you hang on a minute mate, I'm on the eleventh floor. I'll be down in a second anyway. It'll save you coming up."

"Alright, mate," said Norman via the intercom. He was pretty good at disguising his voice. He was absolutely certain this was the one he was after. He had started buzzing all the flats from the top floor down, with the same message. This was the first person that sounded like the twat. Norman walked back to his car and moved it behind the mobile library van that was parked outside the flats. He crept to the left of the block's main entrance where the waste disposal skips were kept and waited.

"Wow, it's massive!" Said K8, staring at the colossal monstrosity of the mobile library. As they moved closer, the driver's door opened and somebody hopped down from the cab. A short man in his mid-twenties faced them. He was a bit overweight for his height, had short mousy hair, and wore glasses. He smiled, exposing teeth that looked like they had been chiselled out of *Wotsits*. "Aw wight, motherfuckers?"

*Oh great,* thought K8, *not only does he have the personal hygiene of a sewer rat but he sounds like Jonathan Ross.*

Ian took the man's right hand in his and they did some intricate hand shaking—a gesture of blokedom. "How's things, Slimer?"

The man appropriately known as Slimer patted Ian on the shoulder. "I'm fine, not been up to much." He looked inquisitively at the other three.

Ian caught on. "Oh, I'm sorry—let me introduce to you my beautiful buxom bombshell, K8." Ian gently put his arm around her. "K8, Slimer, Slimer, K8."

Slimer bowed and kissed her hand. “I’m vewy pleased to meet you."

*Marvellous, now I'll have to disinfect my whole body,* K8 said inwardly.

"And this is my mate Dave, who you've met on numerous occasions and once famously hit because he threw up on your shish kebab."

Dave and Slimer exchanged grunts. Barbarella cut in. "And I'm Barbarella. Pleased to meet you."

Slimer smiled his sleaziest smile. "Enchanted."

Dave cast Slimer an angry look. They’d never got on; Dave reckoned Slimer was a nasty, sleazy, filthy, untrustworthy little ballsack, and on that night he had deliberately aimed for Slimer's kebab.

Slimer loathed Dave right back, mainly because he was so obviously Ian's best mate. He had always been Ian's best mate, but since that hairy little fucker from Suf-fuck had come on the scene, he'd hardly seen him. Oh, and Slimer had spiked Dave's drinks that night with shots of Absinthe so he'd get mind-blowingly bladdered and do something so stupid he'd have to hit him.

Ian saw the tension between his friends and tried to get to the matter at hand. He turned to Slimer and said, "So, have you got them?"

Slimer looked around to see if there was anyone else within earshot. "They're in the van. You got anything to put them in?"

Barbarella looked at K8 with a puzzled appearance, "What are them, then?"

K8 seemed just as clueless. "Beats me."

"Have you brought the bags with you?" Ian asked Dave.

"Oh, for fuck's sake, you never said anything about bags."

"Yes, I did."

"When?"

"Jesus. When I said 'can you bring some bags down?.'"

"Oh... is that what you were on about?"

Ian turned towards the girls and tried to smile his sweetest smile. "Could either of you two lovelies pop up and fetch some bags or a box or something, please?"

"Yeah, sure," said K8, "...how big have they got to be? I mean—what have they got to hold?"

Ian looked around to see if there was anyone about. "Well, it's like this. Slimer here has acquired several bottles of Polish moonshine, and I'm buying some off him."

"Ah," said K8, "and I take it all the secrecy is because it's not exactly the sort you get in Tesco, is it?"

Ian smirked. "You could say that. It's slightly illegal. Now, get up them stairs and get some baggage, please."

K8 extended her hand towards Dave. "Keys, please."

Slimer was looking impatient. "Come on, then." They followed him round to the side of the van and climbed up the steps into the library.

The inside of the van was pretty basic and nowhere near as big as Dave was expecting. There was enough room to get two people side-by-side in the one aisle. Up each side and along the back of the interior were shelves of books. That's all there was to it.

It was like the opposite of the Tardis. Really big on the outside, tiny on the inside. He wondered why the books didn't fall off the shelves when the vehicle was in motion.

Slimer gave him a look. "If you're wondering why the books don't fall off it's because there's a button in the cab that sets up an automatic shelf-edge thingy that keeps the books in place whilst the vehicle is in motion. Dead hi-tech."

Ian frowned. "Oh, I didn't really give a shit, mate."

"Oh," Said Slimer, hurt. "It's what most people say when they come on here, thought I'd get it out the way before you asked."

Dave ignored Slimer and had a look at the selection of books that were on offer. It was all pretty shit. Bollocks, really.

"I'll get the bottles out when your girls get down here; I'm going outside for a smoke." Slimer jumped out the side door.

Dave went to sit in the cab next to Ian. "He's a fuck-pig, you know?"

Ian shrugged. "I don't know what you've got against him, sure he can't pronounce his R's, but he's okay."

"Yeah he might be okay with you and every other person, but he's a right, and left, arsehole with me."

"I don't know, mate. Hey, shall we give him a scare?"

Dave jiggled about in his chair like an over-excited toddler. "What you gonna do?"

Ian started up the van and slipped the gear stick into reverse. They pissed themselves laughing when they heard Slimer's frantic shrieks and stuck their fingers up at him as he screamed at them through the passenger window. All the commotion stopped, though, when they all heard a loud bang and the driver's window exploded.

"Fucking hell," shouted Ian, with glass all over him.

He and Dave watched as Slimer ran around to the front of the van to see what had taken the window out. They were horrified to see the hulking great figure of Norman coming out of from behind a skip, a gun in his hand. They saw Slimer approach him, heard him yell. And then they saw Norman floor him with a whack from the gun.

"Keep driving, for fuck's sake," Dave shouted, jumping into the main library section of the van. He climbed down the steps and pulled the side door shut, stumbling Ian swung the van onto the main road and scraped another vehicle to the sickening screech of metal-on-metal. Ian rammed it into first gear and started down the road. Norman clambered into his car.

"Oh my god. He's gone fucking ballistic," Ian shouted, driving the van past a row of terraced houses. "Where the fuck should we go?"

"I don't know," said Dave. "Just drive."

Ian drove as well as he could. He was only used to cars, although Slimer had let him drive the van a couple of times. He hoped Slimer was okay. He looked in the wing mirror and could see Norman hot on their tail in his little black three-wheeler.

Dave stood in the back of the van trying to think of a way out. They could carry on driving and wait for either the library or Norman to run out of petrol. Or carry on driving and see what the police did. Slimer was bound to call the police. There'd be police helicopters soon, like the ones they show on those CCTV crime programmes.

Ian was amazed to see Norman gaining on them. He took a right turn and sped up a hill. He thanked his instincts that he had told himself to drive away from town. Fewer people to hurt if things went even more tits-up.

## Chapter 12: The Ring Road to Hades

Barbarella moved back from the window, ashen-faced. "Oh my god! We've got to call the police!"

K8 ran to the window and looked down just in time to see the mobile library speeding off into the distance with a three-wheeler close behind.

She saw Slimer lying on the ground. "What the fuck's happened?"

Barbarella explained things in the quickest way possible. "Slimer's-been-fucking-shot-by-fucking-Norman-the-guy-who's-after-Dave-and-he's-chasing-them-up-the-road-in-his-car-and-they're-in-the-mobile-library!"

K8 gasped. "Shitting hell! Have you got your mobile?"

"I left it at my place," said Barbarella, tears welling in her eyes. "Dave's not got his phone, either."

"Shit. We'll have to go down to the call box, then."

The lift seemed to take ages to reach to the eleventh floor and Barbarella couldn't wait any longer. They were wasting too much time. "Oh, fuck this!" She opened the door that led to the stairs and the pair of them bolted down the eleven flights.

K8 shoved open the entrance door, pushing past a couple of teenage girls covered in gold jewellery, one of whom shouted, "Oi, you fucking greebos!"

"Fuck you, princess!" Said Barbarella, and ran after K8. She could still hear the young chavettes mouthing off when she caught up with her at the telephone box. K8 was swearing.

She soon saw why; the telephone box had been vandalised.

"Oh Jesus," Barbarella said. "That's so fucking typical for this town."

"Come on," said K8, jogging across the road. "The next-nearest one is in town."

"Fuck that," Barbarella said "We'll use the phone at my work. It's nearer." They ran down the hill towards The Trough.

"FUCK!" Shrieked Dave and Ian together as they missed an oncoming vehicle by millimetres. Norman had driven alongside the van and had forced them on to the wrong side of the road. The van was swerving all over the road; oncoming vehicles honked their horns and pulled off wherever they could go, out of the way of the library van. Luckily, there wasn't much traffic, but where they were wasn't that built up, just a few houses but mostly fields and trees.

"We need to get him back behind us else we're going to do some serious damage," Cried Ian, trying to floor the van. "This fucking thing's too slow!"

A thought occurred to Dave. *Why not?* It always works in the movies. "Slow down a bit —and try not to jolt us about."

"Slow down? You're joking?"

"No, " Dave shouted, "I'm going to try and get rid of that fuckface. Do what I said."

"What the hell are you gonna do?" Ian's voice was bordering on the hysterical. But he did as he was told.

Dave stumbled down to the middle of the van and reached forward to open the library door. He opened the latch and pushed. It wouldn't open more than an inch because of the force behind it.

Dave went down the steps and pushed the door open with his foot, keeping hold of the bookshelves either side. The door shot open with such a force he thought it may rip from its hinges.

Ian had slowed down so he was level with the opened door.

Dave froze for what seemed like forever as he saw the glaring face of Norman and the barrel of his gun pointing directly at him.

"This is between me and you," Shouted Norman, keeping one eye on the road. "Keep your mate out of it. Stop the van and get out."

Dave hid from view. Maybe he should get Ian to stop? Maybe *bollocks*! He picked a hefty-looking tome from the nearest shelf. "Fuck you!" The book bounced off the roof of Norman's car.

Norman growled and blasted the gun. Dave dove to the floor as the shot blew a hole in the open door.

"Will you fucking let me drive faster now?"

Dave crawled over to the back of Ian's seat. "Where's the moonshine?"

"What?"

"Where's the fucking moonshine?"

Ian thought for a moment. "Have a look in there." He pointed to a metal box behind the passenger seat. Dave opened it and inside were twelve bottles of clear liquid. He unscrewed one of the caps and took a whiff. It smelt really strong; pure alcohol. "Give me your lighter."

Barbarella and K8 stormed into the pub. It was pretty quiet in there, only the usual old drunks and three biker-types sitting in the corner. It was only early evening.

"We need to use your phone," said Barbarella, face wet with tears and streaks of mascara.

The landlord picked up the phone from beneath the bar. "What's the matter?"

Barbarella grabbed the receiver."K8'll tell you."

K8 told the landlord everything, but he already knew about the feud between Dave and Norman. He'd had to pay for the bloody damage.

In the corner, the three biker types (a gigantic legend of a man who called himself Reaper, and his two friends Squizz and Nosher) listened intently. After they had heard everything, Reaper approached the two girls.

Dave and Norman watched as the litre bottle of Polish 'moonshine' with attached lighted rag flew through the air in slow motion.

Dave was really amazed by the accuracy of his first aim. The bottle smashed against the side of Norman's car and the alcohol ignited.

"Motherfucker!" Shouted Ian, as he watched from the wing mirror. Dave wasn't sure if it was a positive or a negative 'motherfucker'.

It was rather rural around there. From Dave's shite geography of the place he had lived for the last few years, he guessed they were on one of the country roads up near Barr Beacon. He was right.

The flaming three-wheeler still kept pace. Norman leaned out of the window again. "Think he's going to take another shot at us," Said Dave.

Ian watched as Norman stuck out the gun and blasted it towards the bottom of the van. "Oh fuck, he's going for the wheels." The first shot didn't hit, and Ian breathed a sigh of relief. "It obviously can't puncture the van, but if he gets lucky and"

"—Look out!" Dave roared, as a number of things happened at once. Up ahead, a car was reversing into a driveway. Ian saw this at the last moment and pulled the steering wheel hard to the right, bumping up over a slight grass verge and into a field. Norman got lucky and blew a hole in one of their rear tyres.

# Chapter 13: The End

John Goode removed his black tie and placed it on the desk before him. He lifted up his mug and drained the last of his hot tea. Eyeing the drinking receptacle for a millisecond he wondered why children always buy their fathers things with golfers on. Either that or it'd be socks and handkerchiefs.

Why do dads always get the crap presents? Mums always receive Belgian chocolates, flowers, vouchers for their favourite shops, or get taken out for a meal. But all dads ever got were socks and handkerchiefs with golfers on, matching mug and sock sets with golfers on, beer tankards with golfers on, or deodorant. With golfers on. Okay, maybe not that last thing. But it wouldn't be surprising. He wished his kids would buy him some book vouchers. John Goode was a real lover of literature.

*

Ian closed his eyes as the van landed with a bump and careered down the hill that had cunningly disguised itself as a field. Dave wasn't in the passenger seat, let alone wearing his seat belt. He was thrown into one of the bookshelves, completely destroying the automatic shelf edges and causing books to fly everywhere.

*

Goode stared across the table at the worn copy of 'Oliver Twist' he had owned since he was eleven years old. He had lost count of how many times he had read it. Reaching into his pocket, he withdrew a bunch of keys, selected one, and pushed it into the lock of a safe that sat beside his desk. He opened the safe and took out a sheet of paper. It was the figures for the shop's takings that month— almost double what it had made in the previous. He smiled. *It goes to show what a little hard work can do,* he said to himself. Over the past month, Goode had had a massive staff meeting, sorted out his staff, and brought them up to scratch. The shop was looking pristine. Head Office had given him permission to employ three more security guards during the day, which meant that hardly any of the regular troublemakers, petty thieves or vandals were let in. Goode shut up the safe, stood, and put on his coat. Picking up his copy of Dickens' classic, which he'd finished re-reading that day, he had the sudden urge to dig out his copy of 'Catcher in the Rye'.

*

J D Salinger's 'Catcher in the Rye' shot out from a bookshelf with immense force, striking a painful blow to Dave's right eye. "Ow! The fuck?"

Ian, meanwhile, was busy wondering whether or not the van would be damaged too much if he drove it through the large barn that sat far away at the bottom of the hill.

Surprisingly, Norman's little three-wheeler was holding up, jumping and jolting after them down the grassy mound.

*

*Although* thought Goode, as he whistled a tune of his own composition, *I feel a bit of a gothic element coming on. Maybe I should dust off my Edgar Allen Poe or get my Lovecraft out?*

*

A red, leather-bound edition of Poe's 'Tales of Mystery and Imagination' struck Dave hard against the side of the head, sending him colliding into the shelves on the opposite side. A swift hit in the stomach by H.P Lovecraft doubled him over.

*

Goode marched through his immaculate store. As he walked down the wines and spirits aisle he considered indulging himself in something else literary. One of the Brontë's would make a nice change, or maybe some George Orwell. *No, I know,* he said to himself as he walked past the cereal, *The Complete Works of William Shakespeare!*

*

Dave was whacked on the head by a rather thick-looking Emily Brontë. He fell to the floor, catching his chin on one of the shelves.

Lying on his front whimpering like a hurt puppy, he wondered why he was so unlucky. All this pain and he could be the one to get in trouble with the police.

A vicious jab to the lower back by George Orwell made him roll on to his back, crying in pain.

Just when he thought he could hurt no more, he watched in sheer unbridled terror as a book of epic proportions teetered on the top shelf above him. 'The Complete Works of...' dropped towards him in a slow, 'Matrix'-style motion, falling, spinning and turning as it fell, landing corner-first upon the left testicle of David Smith. The pain was so unbearable that he took the easy way out and fainted.

*

Goode decided to ditch reading for his entertainment that evening; he would watch television instead. He walked over to the cigarettes and tobacco kiosk to pull down the security shutter.

*

When Dave came to a minute later, he let out a small yelp at the pain in his bollock and clambered to his feet. He climbed into the passenger seat and buckled his seatbelt. Ian was deathly pale and Dave noticed that they seemed to be on the road heading back into town. There was quite a lot of hay stuck to the windscreen wipers and the windscreen. "Mate?"

"Yeah?"

Dave spat what he thought might have been a tooth onto the floor. "Why is there hay all over the van?"

"Barn," said Ian, and erupted into uncontrollable laughter. Dave joined him.

"So, have we lost him?" They both looked into their wing mirrors and could see the menacing shape of The Beast following them, a billowing plume of black smoke coming out of its bonnet.

"No," they said as one. Dave bit his lower lip "Have you thought a way out of this? I haven't."

"Well, my first plan was to either try and lose him or drive until one of us ran out of petrol, but that's not happening. Now I think I should drive straight to the police station. Surely Norman wouldn't be stupid enough to do much there."

Dave dwelled on the idea. "I wouldn't be surprised if he did."

"Oh fuck it, let's risk it, at least they'll be aware of what's happening," Said Ian. "It's about time all this bollocks ended. You never did him any major physical harm."

Dave nodded. "Okay, let's do it."

They drove past their favourite pub, the blown tyre making an irritating flap-flap-flap sound.

*

"You're still here!" Exclaimed Jim Meadows, the last security guard at Tesco. John Goode walked out of the kiosk and grinned at him. "Yes, I'll be off in a second, last-minute procedures and checks— you know me."

Jim chuckled. "So, how are the takings this week?"

Goode's eyes gleamed. "Doubled last month's!"

"Bleeding Ida, you must be doing something right, hey?"

The two men laughed and walked towards the exit.

*

All of a sudden something slammed into the back of the library van, pushing it forward.

"What the fuck's he playing at now?" Cried Dave, looking in the wing mirror. He could see no sign of Norman or his car.

Then: BOOM!

Both men were too busy trying to see what had exploded to notice the dim-witted, chain-smoking, slack-jawed, baseball-capped, youth crossing the road, not giving a fuck if anything was coming.

If he got honked at, he'd tell them to Fuck off, you fucking bastard.

Norman clung to the back of the library. It conveniently had a ladder at the rear. He wept as he watched The Beast give up the ghost as flames devoured it. *It will soon be over,* he thought. *Oh fuck,* he thought next, realising he had left the gun in the car.

"What on Earth's wrong with you? Are you having a heart attack?" Asked Goode, with mild concern. Jim Meadows stood in front of him, looking out through the glass doors. Goode turned and looked over his shoulder at the great big mobile library that came hurtling towards his shop. He grabbed Meadows' left arm and shouted, "Run man, run!"

*

Dave couldn't make out what had blown up, but looked out the window to see the young bloke about fifteen feet ahead of them. "Whoa, look out for the chav," he bellowed. Ian slammed on the brakes. Fortunately, he missed the chav. Unfortunately? Not Tesco.

*

The library crashed through the glass doors, ploughing through the fruit and veg aisles. Goode managed to get himself and Jim Meadows out of the way in time. They landed in a heap, watching in disbelief as the van destroyed everything in its path before one of the five-metre freezers slowed it down and it finally screeched to a noisy halt.

The first thing Dave saw when he opened his eyes was a jar of mayonnaise. The windscreen had imploded and he and Ian were covered in tiny squares of glass. "Ian?" His friend was slumped over the steering wheel, not moving. Dave quickly unbuckled his seat belt and leaned across to see if he was okay. "Ian, mate?" It wasn't the most sensible thing to do, but Dave shook him. "Oh no!" Dave whimpered as Ian's body fell on him. Why does a person instantly become referred to a body when they're dead? "Oh, fucking hell." Dave cradled Ian's head in his arms. "It's all my fault, all my fault." Tears rained down onto Ian's face.

"Oh, that's sooo original, you fucking girl."

Dave opened his blurry eyes and looked down at Ian's face. He was smiling up at him.

"Thank god you're alive; I was just about to perform an act of necrophilia!"

Ian sat up quickly and laughed. "You sick cunt."

Suddenly the passenger door opened and a furious voice shouted. "You!"

Goode grabbed Dave and yanked him out of the van, flinging him to the tiled floor.

Dave hit the floor hard and cowered in the shadow of the looming figure of John Goode. Never had he ever seen him this angry.

"You worthless, useless little piece of shit. I suppose you and your lowlife boyfriend stole this vehicle. You make me sick, born to be a lazy good-for-nothing waste of space." Goode pulled off his jacket and threw it to the floor. "Well, I'm going to show you."

Dave moved back across the floor on his backside. The look of horror upon his face reached a new height when he saw Norman appear from behind the van. Goode, who was oblivious to Norman's presence, took hold of Dave's t-shirt and lifted him off the floor, throwing him against one of the checkout counters. Dave's arm flopped out and hit something that started the conveyor belt. "Oh shit," Dave cursed aloud when he tried to lift his head. A large chunk of his hair was trapped. He was stuck.

Maniacal laughter echoed throughout the shop.

Goode turned to see Norman in hysterics. "Oh, and I suppose you're the silly fucker who was driving?" Marching up to him, knowing Dave wasn't going anywhere, he filled with more rage. "What is it with you lot? Look at you, you filthy fat bastard."

Norman looked away from his target for a second and seized Goode by the shirt collar, and head-butted him in the face.

Goode fell to the floor holding his bloodied, now-broken nose.

"Ian?" Dave screamed, jerking his head up and wincing in pain.

Norman approached. "Looks like it's just you and me." He reached around and pulled out a six-inch flick knife from his back pocket, pressing the button.

*Fuck, fuck, fuck,* said Dave's inner voice as he pulled at his hair with both hands. It wouldn't budge. Norman held his kicking legs down and straddled his waist. Dave beat at Norman with his fists but Norman caught one of his arms and trapped it against his knee. He did the same with the other one. Dave was helpless. The foul halitosis of Norman was inches away from his face. "'s alright, mate. I'm only going to stab you."

*Oh, well, that's reassuring,* thought Dave. He did the last thing he could think of as he felt the cold blade against his throat. He kissed Norman passionately on the mouth. Norman frowned, completely confused for a moment. Then Dave bit down as hard as he could on his assailant's lower lip and shoved a knee into his groin.

Norman yelled out in pain and punched Dave hard in the face. He raised the knife high.

"STOP, VIPER!" Came a deep, god-like voice.

Norman and Dave both froze.

Standing by the side of the mobile library were about a dozen Hell's Angels, with Barbarella, K8 and Ian. The deep booming voice had come from the giant of an angel called Reaper.

"What did you say?" Asked Norman.

Reaper stared at him out of intense black eyes. "I said 'stop, Viper!' Put the knife down!"

Norman did as instructed; even he wasn't foolish enough to argue with Reaper.

"Get off him."

Norman climbed down and stood still as if waiting to be commanded.

"Look at him, Norman. What has this child done that has given you a reason to take out such an extreme act of vengeance?"

Norman looked down at his feet, ashamed.

Reaper continued. "Don't you see he is on our side?"

Norman didn't know what the hell Reaper was going on about; neither did Dave.

"He is one of us, Norman, and so is Ian."

Norman frowned. "What do you mean?"

Reaper looked at Norman sincerely. "I am Ian's father."

Gasps came from all around. A couple of Angels who had found the alcohol aisle choked on their beer.

Norman was wide-eyed. "Then why the fuck didn't you help them out during that fight in the pub?"

Reaper smiled. "I have watched over him for years without his knowledge. I know he can take care of himself. And besides, I did help in a way."

"How?"

"I passed my daughter Barbarella the fire extinguisher."

A series of gasps came from the crowd, the biggest from Barbarella and Ian.

"Let me explain," began Reaper. "I have had many, many women, from many, many towns and places, and I vowed never to settle in one place no matter what."

"But after finding out I created these two here," he said, waving towards Ian and Barbarella, "a rather paternal side came over me and I have stayed here ever since, watching over them without their knowledge."

Norman mulled this over and after a minute or so said, "So why can't I kill him?" pointing at Dave.

Reaper laughed. "You can."

A large chorus of *Noooo* rang out.

"But if you do, whilst you're serving a life sentence, you'll miss out on riding with us."

Norman's eyes lit up. "You mean...?"

Reaper nodded and turned to a completely bald Angel. "Tampon, give it here."

Tampon handed over a denim jacket with the sleeves ripped off. "Welcome to the Wasters, Norman, or should I say Viper."

Tears of joy sprang to Norman's eyes as he put on his own personal biker jacket.

"Also..."Reaper began, "Thrush, bring on the big one." Another Angel disappeared behind the van. "Because of the tragic demise of The Beast, we thought this would comfort you a little. Behold, The Demon!"

The crowd parted to reveal the angel Thrush pushing along an immaculate purple Harley Davidson with 'Demon' painted on its fuel tank.

Norman burst into big wet girly tears.

Reaper put an arm around him. "There, there, let it all out. You're one of us now. But...."

Norman looked up at the awesome face of Reaper. "But what?"

"As a member of The Wasters, you must help and watch over all of our friends and family as we will do yours. We are all one body now. Prick one of us, and we all hurt."

Norman didn't need telling twice. "Oh, alright then."

"Oh great, a great big gang of hairy fucking twats," Shouted the reawakened, slightly delirious Goode. As eighteen sets of eyes gave him evil glares, he noticed Jim Meadows sharing an Angel's beer.

"Umm... is there room for one more?"

With that, everybody left the wreckage of the supermarket and went down to the best pub in the universe for some serious drinking, a knees-up, and a chippy tea.

## Epilogue: The Future

Dave goes back to university and studies English and becomes a horror writer, out-selling Stephen King. He has three children with Barbarella who they named Thora, Bramble, and Dickinson.

Ian joins The Wasters and becomes a younger image of his new-found father. He and K8 spend years and years together before K8 actually confesses to being a bit of a lesbian. He now lives in a house near Birmingham with K8 and their lesbian lover, much to Dave's chagrin.

Norman goes on to be a vital member of The Wasters and devotes all his time to them. Sadly, after fifty-seven years, he falls asleep at the handlebars whilst at a rally in Dover and gets buried somewhere in the British Channel.

John Goode is eventually promoted to head of the company and ends up living long enough to see Tesco stores open worldwide.

Slimer is never seen again but nobody really liked him anyway as he was a filthy twat who couldn't pronounce his 'R's'.

The sexy naked lesbians in custard disappeared from Dave's dreams as soon as he had slept with Barbarella and as an annual treat for his birthdays, she submerges herself in a paddling pool of custard purely for his consumption.

Dave's parents find out about the real Dave and love him just as much as the Dave he pretended to be.

The Trough finally gets demolished in the year 6009, surviving three apocalypses and seventeen world wars.

**Author Biography**

Matthew Cash, or Matty-Bob Cash, as he is known to most, was born and raised in Suffolk, which is the setting for his debut novel, Pinprick. He is compiler and editor of Death by Chocolate, a chocoholic horror anthology, and the 12Days Anthology, head of Burdizzo Books and Burdizzo Bards, and has numerous releases on Kindle and several collections in paperback.

He has always written stories since he first learned to write, and most, although not all, tend to slip into the many-layered murky depths of the Horror genre.

His influences —from childhood to present day— include: Roald Dahl, James Herbert, Clive Barker, Stephen King, and Stephen Laws, to name but a few.

More recently, he enjoys the work of Adam Nevill, F.R Tallis, Michael Bray, Gary Fry, William Meikle and Iain Rob Wright (who featured Matty-Bob in his famous A-Z of Horror title, M is For Matty-Bob, plus Matthew wrote his own version of events, which was included as a bonus).

He is a father of two, a husband of one, and a zookeeper of numerous fur babies.

You can find him here:
www.facebook.com/pinprickbymatthewcash
https://www.amazon.co.uk/-/e/B010MQTWKK

Matthew Cash

## PINPRICK

All villages have their secrets, and Brantham is no different.

Twenty-years ago, after foolish risk-taking turned into tragedy, Shane left the rural community under a cloud of suspicion and rumour. Events from that night remain unexplained, memories erased, questions unanswered. Now a notorious politician, he returns to his birthplace when the offer from a property developer is too good to refuse. With big plans to haul Brantham into the 21st century, the developers have already made a devastating impact on the once quaint village. But then the headaches begin, followed by the nightmarish visions.

Soon, Shane wishes he had never returned, as Brantham reveals its ugly secret.

## VIRGIN AND THE HUNTER

Hi, I'm God. And I have a confession to make.

I live with my two best friends and the girl of my dreams, Persephone.

When opportunity knocks, we are usually down the pub having a few drinks, or we'll hang out in Christchurch Park until it gets dark, then go home to do college stuff. Even though I struggle a bit financially, life is good, carefree.

Well, it was.

Things have started going downhill recently, from the moment I started killing people.

**KRACKERJACK**

Five people wake up in a warehouse, bound to chairs.

Before each of them, tacked to the wall, are their witness testimonies.

They each played a part in labelling one of Britain's most loved family entertainers a paedophile and sex offender.

Clearly, revenge is the reason they have been brought here, but the man they accused is supposed to be dead.

Opportunity knocks, and Diddy Dave Diamond has one last game show to host —and it's a knockout.

**KRACKERJACK2**

Ever wondered what would happen if a celebrity faked their own death and decided they had changed their minds?

Two years ago, publicly shunned comedian Diddy Dave Diamond convinced the nation that he was dead, only to return from beyond the grave to seek retribution on those who ruined his career and tainted his legacy.

Innocent or not, only one person survived Diddy Dave Diamond's last ever game show, but the forfeit prize was imprisonment for similar alleged crimes.

Prison is not kind to inmates with those type of convictions, as the sole survivor finds out, but there's a sudden glimmer of hope.

Someone has surfaced in the public eye claiming to be the dead comedian.

**FUR**

The old-aged pensioners of Boxford are very set in their ways, loyal to each other and their daily routines. With families and loved ones either moved on to pastures new or maybe even the next life, these folk can become dependent on one another.

But what happens when the natural ailments of old age begin to take their toll?

What if they were given the opportunity to heal, and overcome the things that make everyday life less tolerable?

What if they were given this ability without their consent?

When a group of local thugs attack the village's wealthy Victor Krauss, they unwittingly create a maelstrom of events that not only could destroy their home but everyone in and around it.

Are the old folk the cause or the cure of the horrors?

## KEIDA-IN-THE-FLAMES

Zoë just wants to go home after a hard week of work. Netflix, pyjamas, and junk food beckon. The prospect of catching the last bus is always daunting but seven days of relaxation and revision seem like a worthy prize at the end of another journey of drunken idiots, weed clouds and loud unwanted music. But there's someone special on board, what starts as an act of human kindness descends into a madness more viscous and evil than she could ever imagine.

## Other Releases by Matthew Cash

**Novels**
Virgin and the Hunter
Pinprick

**Novellas**
Ankle Biters
KrackerJack
KrackerJack 2
Clinton Reed's Fat
Illness
Hell and Sebastian
Waiting for Godfrey
Deadbeard
The Cat Came Back
Frosty [coming 2019]
**Short Stories**
Why Can't I Be You?
Slugs and Snails and Puppydog Tails
OldTimers
Hunt the C*nt
Keida-in-the-flames

**Non-fiction**
From Whale-Boy to Aqua-man

**Anthologies Compiled and Edited by Matthew Cash of Burdizzo Books**
Death by Chocolate
12 Days STOCKING FILLERS
12 Days: 2016
12 Days: 2017
The Reverend Burdizzo's Hymnbook*

SPARKS*
Under the Weather [ with Em Dehaney & Back Road Books]
Burdizzo Mix Tape Vol.1*
*with Em Dehaney

**Anthologies Featuring Matthew Cash**
Rejected for Content 3: Vicious Vengeance
JEApers Creepers
Full Moon Slaughter
Full Moon Slaughter 2
Down the Rabbit Hole: Tales of Insanity
Visions from the Void [edited by Jonathan Butcher & Em Dehaney]

**Collections**
The Cash Compendium Volume One
The Cash Compendium Continuity
Come and Raise Demons [poetry]

Website:
www.Facebook.com/pinprickbymatthewcash

Printed in Great Britain
by Amazon

58596436R00071